A

THE PINTO RIDER

Broken Arrow was a quiet town situated near the border between Texas and Mexico. Quiet, that is, until the arrival of Zococa, the famed bandit, and his sidekick Tahoka, the giant, mute Apache warrior. When an old rancher friend of Zococa's enlists his help to find out what is happening on the Double X Ranch, Zococa leaps into action. As a deadly battle erupts all around the duo, neither knows that there is even more danger on his trail . . .

MICHAEL D. GEORGE

THE PINTO RIDER

Complete and Unabridged

LINFORD
Leicester

First published in Great Britain in 2002 by
Robert Hale Limited
London

First Linford Edition
published 2003
by arrangement with
Robert Hale Limited
London

British Library CIP Data

George, Michael D.
  The pinto rider.—Large print ed.—
  Linford western library
  1. Western stories
  2. Large type books
  I. Title
  823.9'14 [F]

  ISBN 1–8439–5079–0

Published by
F. A. Thorpe (Publishing)
Anstey, Leicestershire

Set by Words & Graphics Ltd.
Anstey, Leicestershire
Printed and bound in Great Britain by
T. J. International Ltd., Padstow, Cornwall

This book is printed on acid-free paper

Dedicated to legendary cowboy star,
Monte Hale

Prologue

Luis Santiago Rodrigo Vallencio was never one to shun the attention of others. He had always wanted to be famous and had worked hard to achieve his goal. Yet he had somehow managed to achieve his ambition at a cost most rational men would have never been willing to pay.

But he had paid the price willingly, for life was to him nothing more than an amusing game. Not something to be taken seriously.

In fact, he had never taken anything too seriously. Not even being branded a notorious bandit and hunted for the bounty others had put upon his head.

Wanted Dead or Alive on both sides of the border, the handsome left-handed bandit known simply as Zococa, still enjoyed the admiration of the majority of females he encountered.

This for Zococa, was why he had chosen his colourful if dangerous profession.

Yet unlike the thousands of stories which had grown around the famed Zococa, he was not the ruthless killer he joyfully bragged himself to be. He had never killed anyone who had not required killing.

His exploits were mostly the work of his agile tongue, for he had never been one to stop talking whenever there was a willing or captive audience.

To him, an audience could be just one listener.

Zococa's philosophy was simple.

Why tell someone that you have robbed one bank when you could tell him you have robbed hundreds? Why tell people that you have never shot anyone with the prized pistol in cold blood, when you could boast of shooting thousands? There was only one thing the handsome bandit had never been forced to exaggerate about and that was his success with the fairer sex. For it seemed that most of them were inexplicably drawn to the elegant Zococa by some invisible force.

Zococa seemed unable to stop talking as long as there was someone there to listen. As Zococa rode his magnificent pinto stallion back and forth across the long border which separated Texas from Mexico, he had his captive audience always riding beside him.

Tahoka was a giant Apache warrior. He rode with the Mexican bandit at all times. They had become like brothers and yet some had noticed how Zococa tended to treat his constant companion more like a son. Having been tortured beyond the limits of most normal men's endurance, the Apache's life had been saved by the handsome pinto rider. Tahoka's tongue had been torn from his mouth, leaving him mute. Other atrocities had been done to the Indian which had left him unlike other men. He owed his life to the always smiling Mexican.

Tahoka knew he could never repay this debt. Even being drawn into the life of a hunted bandit did nothing to deter the Apache warrior's loyalty for his ever-smiling friend. Theirs was a bond like no other.

The Indian used the sign language he had learned as a young warrior to talk with his younger more flamboyant friend, but seldom managed to interrupt the continuous verbal outbursts for long. Zococa had learned to read the hand signals of his enormous pal quickly and yet still managed to start and finish both sides of their conversations.

Tahoka's life had been saved by the notorious Mexican, yet the bandit never seemed to talk about this gallant deed but favoured exaggerating other lesser exploits. Most of which were pure fiction and the product of his fertile imagination.

Why? Because exaggeration was his forte. As was his ability to never take anything seriously. He lived for the moment and the moment was for living.

To be doing nothing was to Zococa little better than being dead. His life had to be filled with danger and the thrill of outwitting each and every one of his enemies.

Some ambitious bounty hunters had seen the Wanted posters and decided to try and claim the reward money on Zococa's handsome head. They judged the book by its cover. They saw the silver thread woven into his sombrero. The silver pistol in the hand-tooled holster. The smiling tanned face with the thin black moustache. How could this sort of man actually be able to defend himself against hardened bounty hunters?

Zococa had taught them all a lesson.

For all his handsome looks and his immaculate clothes, Zococa was indeed an expert with the silver-plated Colt he wore on his left hip.

This was a fact they learned to their cost.

None had ever managed to outdraw the Mexican bandit.

To the law he had become someone they wanted dead by any means. Zococa had become an embarrassment to the authorities of both Texas and Mexico.

Not because he had actually done the incredible things he had bragged about, but because they believed that the infamous reputation Zococa had created around himself was true.

But why would an intelligent young man seek the danger of being a wanted outlaw? Some said it was because he actually was as ruthless as he claimed to be. Others, who had met the elegant Mexican, knew the true reason.

A famed bandit such as Zococa was someone who was respected and feared by the criminal element which could be found in any town, however big or small. This gave Zococa the danger his nature craved, but there was another reason: one which satisfied the romantic side of the bandit. He was always welcome in the arms of admiring females everywhere he went.

There had been so many beautiful women who had yearned for him to climb up to their balconies and make love to them. And so many who had fulfilled their ambition.

They say God smiles upon the pure of heart and protects them against all who try to do them harm. So it was with Zococa as he rode from one adventure to another with his silent companion always at his side.

For whatever Zococa claimed to be, he was in reality the most noble of souls and as a result lived a charmed life. Always willing to risk everything for those less able than himself to protect themselves.

Few men deliberately seek to make themselves famous if the cost of that fame is so high. Yet the rider of the magnificent pinto stallion cared little for his own safety. All he had ever wanted was to become a famous bandit.

He had succeeded gloriously.

Yet none of his enemies or even his admirers knew the name of Luis Santiago Rodrigo Vallencio.

To them, he was simply Zococa. The left-handed one.

1

Colonel Orlando Fernandez was a man on a mission. He had been sent from Mexico City to locate and kill the notorious bandit known simply as Zococa. For more than a decade the famed Zococa had ridden in and out of Texas until his escapades had become an embarrassment to the fragile Mexican government. If there was ever going to be a reconciliation between the two very different countries that graced each side of the seemingly endless border, it was deemed prudent that bandits like Zococa should be eliminated.

Fernandez was no mere hired killer or even a bounty hunter though. His was a higher calling. For seventeen years he had served as a bodyguard to the Emperor's family and had ascended to the illustrious rank of colonel.

Fernandez had never been found wanting when the yardstick was courage or ability.

The expert horseman, duellist and marksman had been hand-picked by those in authority for this secret mission. It was known that Zococa was well thought of throughout Mexico and eliminating him would have to be done with the utmost care. It would have to appear that the bandit simply ran out of luck at the hands of one who was just a little faster on the draw than himself.

There was none more capable of executing his orders in all of Mexico than Orlando Fernandez. If Zococa was to be got rid of swiftly, he was the only man who could do it. There was to be no link with the government. So Fernandez had exchanged his uniform for the wardrobe of a travelling gentleman. The two soldiers who accompanied him would be, to all intents and purposes, his loyal servants.

Riding with two personally chosen

soldiers, Jose Remo and Carlos Concisco, the tall Orlando Fernandez cut
a fine figure as they had driven north
toward the small Mexican border
town of San Pueblo. A town known as
one often frequented by the elusive
bandit and his constant companion,
Tahoka.

Even in the distant Mexico City,
news had reached the ears of the
dictatorship that San Pueblo was
probably one of Zococa's favourite
hideouts. Situated high on a mountain-
side and surrounded by dense
woodland, the small Mexican town was
rumoured to be a place where the
famed bandit often sought refuge.

Fernandez had been riding with his
two cohorts for more than three weeks
when they had finally spotted the
buildings balanced on the side of the
mountain. They stopped their mounts
and stared in awe at the town above
them. It was situated a mere five miles
from the river border, just as their
information had said. The morning

11

sun bathed the whitewashed buildings perched on the side of the high mountain in all its glory.

The tall rider dismounted and signalled to Remo and Concisco to do the same. All three men studied the narrow twisting trail which appeared to be the only safe route up to the town.

'Should we rest, Señor Fernandez?' Remo asked the tall figure who checked his arsenal of weaponry strapped to the back of a pack-horse.

'There will be plenty of time to rest, Jose,' Fernandez answered powerfully.

'But the horses are weary,' Concisco pointed out as he moved between their mounts and the three packhorses.

Fernandez nodded, '*Sí*. They are weary, but this is no time to worry ourselves about such things.'

'When will you tell us the details of our secret mission, Señor Fernandez?' Carlos Concisco asked fearfully.

Orlando Fernandez glanced at both

his companions in turn before speaking.

'Now is as good a time as any, Carlos.'

Both men stood to attention and listened carefully to their leader.

'We are here to find the bandit Zococa. When we have found him, we will kill him and take his head back to the Emperor's palace. We will be rewarded with gold enough to last a dozen lifetimes.'

'But Zococa is said to have killed a hundred men.' Concisco swallowed hard.

'I have killed more, Carlos.' Fernandez smiled.

Jose Remo moved closer to the emotionless man who was removing a silver flask from his long coat and unscrewing its stopper.

'Do you think Zococa is up there, *Señor?*'

Fernandez took a mouthful of brandy and savoured its flavour as it warmed his innards. It was the only link he still had to the civilized life he had led for so many years in the service of his emperor.

'We should find out in roughly an hour, Jose.'

Remo and Concisco watched their leader hold on to his saddle horn and step into his stirrup before mounting the tall horse. They quickly returned to their own horses and scrambled back on to their saddles.

'We shall ride slowly to San Pueblo, my friends,' Fernandez said as he jabbed his spurs into the flesh of his horse and headed towards the trail. 'We shall give them plenty of time to hide the vermin who have brought shame to Mexico. But they will not be able to hide their horses as easily.'

'Horses?' Concisco questioned.

'*Sí*, Carlos. Our intelligence service has discovered many things about the bandit who calls himself Zococa. He rides a magnificent pinto stallion. A horse which I shall own when this is all over.' Fernandez grinned.

'What other things do we know about

this bandit?' Remo asked with a curiosity not usual in the short thickset man.

'He rides with a savage. A dirty stinking Indian who is said to be bigger than normal men. This savage rides a black gelded mount.'

'What sort of person rides with a filthy Indian, *Señor*?'

'Only the worst sort of creature, my friend.' Fernandez took another swallow as he rode up the steep trail into the cooling shade of countless tress.

'Zococa.' Remo spat.

'*Sí*, amigo. Zococa.'

★ ★ ★

The three riders entered San Pueblo just before noon. The streets, paved with thousands of stones, echoed with the sound of their mounts' hoofs and those of the trailing pack animals. Yet for all the noise they made as they entered the small town perched on the side of the great mountain, they saw nobody.

'This is strange, *amigo*,' Jose Remo said as he drew one of his lethal pistols from its holster and cocked its hammer.

'I do not like it,' Concisco added.

'Do not fret, my friends,' Fernandez said as his eyes darted around the strange scenery. He had spotted more than a dozen fearful eyes hiding behind walls and wooden shutters.

'But the town is empty,' Remo said.

'Not empty, Jose. Far from empty,' the tall rider said as he pulled back on his reins and swiftly dismounted outside a solid structure with the word CANTINA painted on its white wall.

The two followers slid off their own horses and moved between the animals up to the hitching rail where Fernandez stood studying the street carefully.

'We are being watched by many eyes, *amigos*.'

The two men tied all their animals to the hitching rails before finally ducking beneath the long wooden poles and stepping to Fernandez's side.

'Where are they all?'

'All around us.' Fernandez waved his hand to indicate all the faces he had noticed hiding from view. Then he spotted something near the corner of the building before them. He stepped down on to the rough ground from the carved-stone walkway and began to nod to himself. Remo and Concisco followed their leader as he investigated.

'Look.'

Remo and Concisco moved to his side and stared at the black-and-white horse standing in the shade, flicking its tail at the flies which were attracted to it. It had a fine saddle and looked well cared for. It fitted the description perfectly.

'The pinto stallion!' Carlos exclaimed excitedly.

'*Sí*, Carlos. We have found the stallion, now we have to find its master.' Fernandez smiled as he flicked the safety loops off his pair of exquisite pistols.

The three men turned and readied their weaponry as they walked the dozen paces back to the beaded curtain hanging in the cantina's door frame.

'Come, *amigos*,' Fernandez said as he led his companions into the cantina and studied the three occupants.

One was an elderly woman who seemed to work mainly behind the bar. Another was a man in his forties who seemed to do nothing except feed the stove with wood as he tried to create enough heat inside its oven to start cooking. The third was a man who leaned on the bar counter with his back to the three intruders. He was lean and dressed in tight fitting black clothes. His sombrero was decorated with silver thread. On his hip he wore a single gun which sat in a hand-tooled holster on a black detailed belt.

Colonel Fernandez indicated to his two companions to move to either side of him as he flexed his fingers above his white pearl-handled gun-grips.

'Turn around, *amigo*,' Fernandez commanded the man.

'Why, *señor*?' the man asked as he

finished his tequila and placed the empty glass down on the surface of the wooden counter.

'Because I have told you to do so,' Fernandez snapped again as he nodded for his men to start pulling their own weapons from their holsters. Remo and Concisco quietly drew their guns and aimed at the seemingly defiant figure.

'Draw, Zococa,' Fernandez shouted.

Swiftly the man turned to face the colonel. His gun flashed from its holster at a speed none of the trio had expected. The pistol fired once before Fernandez had cleared his own holsters with his pair of guns. Bullets blasted from the Colts of Concisco and Remo.

Fernandez fired again and again with a precision only a man of military training could have managed. The small cantina became enveloped in black gun-smoke.

In the choking darkness the sound of a man hitting the ground echoed off the solid walls.

For more than two minutes nobody

within the cantina moved a muscle as they waited fearfully for the air to clear enough for them to see the result of their handiwork.

Orlando Fernandez started moving first. His eyes were focused on the floor where the man lay, still holding on to his pistol. Remo edged forward and kicked the gun from the lifeless fingers.

'We did it, *señor*. We killed Zococa.'

Fernandez holstered his guns and strode across to the body, which was riddled with bullets.

'This is not Zococa.' His words seemed to hang on the stale air inside the cantina.

'I do not understand, *amigo*,' Concisco said drily.

'This man was right-handed.' Fernandez pointed at the body and the outstretched right arm and the holster on the right hip. 'We have killed the wrong man. This is not Zococa.'

'But the pinto stallion outside?' Remo remonstrated.

Fernandez's eyes flashed at both his men.

'There must be many men with such fine animals, my friends.'

'But why did he fight?'

'I think we did not give him many choices.' Fernandez stared at the old woman behind the bar. Her face was rigid with fear as her hands pushed the half-full bottle of tequila towards him.

'What do we do now?' Remo asked as he slid his gun into its holster.

'We drink. We eat. We ride.'

2

It had started three nights earlier. Someone claimed to have spotted an elegant Mexican riding a huge pinto stallion in the vicinity of Broken Arrow, a small Texan town situated near the river border to Mexico. That information alone might have raised little interest in the quiet town had it not been for the additional information concerning the Mexican's unusual riding companion. The news that there was a huge Apache who rode with the Mexican suddenly made everyone with a gun, and a horse, within twenty miles taste reward money in the air.

For although nobody had ever seen a photographic likeness of Zococa and only had artists' impressions of the bandit on the Wanted posters to go by, it was known that he never rode anywhere without his Indian companion, Tahoka.

The thought of having such a notorious pair of bandits somewhere in or around the small town of Broken Arrow had brought out the posse. The posse, which drove deeper and deeper into the fragrant Mexican woods, totalled more than twenty in number. They were led by Sheriff Tobius Randall, a portly figure with a grey moustache that covered most of his face. He sported white sheepskin chaps that were better suited to a less ferocious climate and a cattle-hide vest that did nothing to disguise his beer belly. For the third time in as many nights the posse had been lured across the shallow river and ridden south of the border from the sleepy Texan town of Broken Arrow.

The posse had been riding around in circles for over an hour and tempers were frayed as they stopped at the river and allowed their exhausted mounts to drink.

For three consecutive nights the strange array of riders had followed the sheriff as he in turn followed the dust of the two bandits.

They were being taunted by Zococa and Tahoka.

At first the posse was like hounds on the scent of a fox, but now it seemed as if it were they themselves who were being chased.

They were chasing their own shadows, and they knew it.

It was strange for anyone in the quiet town to do anything on the daring side, but this, they were told by Sheriff Randall, was different. This was their chance to put Broken Arrow on the map by catching the notorious Mexican bandit, Zococa. It would also be a profitable exercise if they succeeded. For the cash-strapped Texans, who made up the posse, even a few dollars were worth risking their lives for.

Yet they were no closer now than they had been when they had started. It was like chasing phantoms.

Randall lowered his canteen into the cold river and allowed it to fill before hoisting it back up and taking a much-needed drink.

'I figure we're damn close now, boys. We got them cornered now for sure.'

'Where is he, Toby? I'm damn sore,' the local newspaper man named Jonas Quaid asked, standing in his stirrups and rubbing his buttocks.

'Quit belly-aching, Jonas,' Randall snapped as water dripped from his moustache. 'We'll catch the critters and have that reward money for ourselves.'

'We ain't ever gonna catch that Mex or his Injun friend.' The barber named Felix Snape spat into the fast flowing water that licked at their horses' legs.

'That's defeatism. I'm not having none of you boys thinking thataway. We are gonna catch them both,' Sheriff Randall shouted at the smaller rider.

'I don't like it,' Wally Beer said with an honesty found only in those of a superstitious nature. 'It's unlucky to be riding around in the light of the moon, when it's over your left shoulder.'

'What?' Randall pushed his hat off his sweating hairline and tried to work out Beer's statement.

'Wally's in one of his doom and death moods again,' Jonas Quaid said.

'You might mock but I heard tell of a posse that rode around in the moonlight and they all got the fever.' Wally nodded at his fellow riders.

'What kind of fever, Wally?' Felix Snape asked.

'It might have been black or it might have been yellow or then again it might have been swamp,' Wally replied looking over his shoulder at the moon.

'Was you drinking before we lit out from town, Wally?' the sheriff asked the bumbling rider.

'Nope. Not a drop has touched my lips all day.' Beer waved his hands around as he studied the moon over his shoulder again.

'You mean you're sober and still talking like a loco bean?'

'You might mock but I don't mock

the ways of the unknown.'

Felix Snape aimed his mount at the Texan side of the river.

'That's it. I've had enough eyewash for one night. I'm gonna go back to my shop and find me a drop of whiskey to drink.'

Tobius Randall spurred his horse until it caught up with the barber. He grabbed hold of Snape's sleeve.

'Don't quit now. We must be getting darn close to the bastards.'

Snape pulled back on his reins and looked at the faces of his fellow posse members. Even in the light of the moon he could see they all wanted to join him. Yet unlike himself, they were afraid of the burly sheriff.

'Admit it, Toby. We've chased them *hombres* for three nights in a row and we ain't even caught a glimpse of anything 'cepting their dust. Let's get home and rest up.'

Randall waved his finger under the nose of the barber.

'I ought to thrash you, Felix.'

Faster than the lawman could blink, Snape pulled a straight razor from his vest pocket and held its honed edge to the throat of Randall.

'You forget, Toby, I'm your barber and at least four times a week you put that fat throat of yours in my hands. I'd hate for me to be so sleepy that I accidentally chopped some important part of your body off.'

Randall carefully pushed the razor away from his face and then cleared his throat.

'Felix is right, men. We better call it a night. That Zococa varmint is probably miles away from here by now anyway.'

The riders trailed across the river and then headed back towards Broken Arrow. There was an air of gloom over the posse as it gathered pace when the lights of the distant buildings came into view through the trees.

No one seemed to see anything except their homes and businesses stretched out before them. If they had just looked over their shoulders at the trail behind them, they would have seen the huge Apache rider sitting astride his black gelding, silently following them with the reins of the riderless pinto stallion in his hands.

Tahoka had led the posse a merry dance around the countryside for hours, knowing that his partner, Zococa, was in the heart of Broken Arrow. And had been, since the posse had ridden out earlier that night.

3

'You are the most beautiful thing I have ever set eyes upon, my darling,' Zococa said into the ear of the female he had in his arms. When the posse had ridden out of town chasing Tahoka's deliberate dust, the handsome bandit had carefully walked the streets of Broken Arrow trying to work out which of the two banks was the easier to rob. Then, passing along a narrow alley filled with fragrant rose-vines that stretched up the sides of a dozen whitewashed buildings, he had spotted a female. She had been standing on the small balcony trimmed with black wrought-iron railings watching the sun setting.

Perhaps it was the crimson light that illuminated her face and long dark hair that Zococa had noticed first. It might have been the way her white cotton dress clung tightly to her upper body and made her heaving bosom seem so inviting. Whatever the reason was for his stopping, he did so willingly.

'Hello, my little one,' Zococa had called up to the balcony.

She, like a quarter of the population of the border town, was of Mexican origin. She had leaned over the balcony and smiled when her eyes glimpsed the handsome features of the man who held his sombrero across his heart.

'Who are you, *señor*?'

'I am the humble villain you have enslaved with your beauty,' Zococa replied with a flash of his perfect teeth.

'What is your name?'

'They call me Zococa.'

'Zococa?' She gripped the railing tightly and gazed down at the figure bathed in the light of a solitary street lantern. 'The bandit?'

'*Sí*, my ravishing one.' Zococa studied the vine which clung to the side of the building. It was sturdy. 'May I come to you?'

She began to blush.

'But what would the great Zococa want with me?'

Zococa laughed and threw his sombrero up into the air. She caught it and watched silently as he climbed up after it. Reaching the balcony, he held on to the wrought-iron railings and then smiled again.

'What is your name?' he asked.

'My name is Rita, Zococa,' she replied, holding the brim of his large black sombrero in her small hands. It seemed to shield her entire body from his prying eyes. A situation he would soon remedy.

With the grace of an athlete, Zococa jumped from the branches and landed on the balcony directly in front of her. His hands peeled the sombrero away from her and dropped it on to the tiled floor at their feet.

'Rita is such a wonderful name, my little one,' Zococa had said in a low breathless tone which made her lick her red shining lips.

'We must be quiet, Zococa. My

mother and father are downstairs in the parlour.' Rita looked up into the smiling face which towered above her. She had heard so many tales of the great bandit but had never imagined that one day he would seek her favours in such a romantic fashion.

Zococa nodded as his eyes wandered down over her exquisite body. Her waist was narrow and her hips just slightly wider but it was her breasts which heaved beneath the white cotton blouse that seemed so perfect.

He moved slowly toward her and she backed away until she felt the cool wall stopping her retreat. Zococa glanced inside the room through the open balcony door. It was a nice room. Neat with all the little things young females instinctively gather about themselves. When he had located the bed, he looked back into her eyes.

'Oh, Rita. You have speared my very heart with your beauty.'

'I did nothing,' she said honestly.

'You looked down upon my humble

being and dragged me up here merci-lessly, but I forgive you.' Zococa rested one arm on the wall and toyed with her perfect chin with his free hand.

'Why are you in Broken Arrow, Zococa?'

Zococa touched his lips with his index finger as his brain raced. Since spotting her, he had quite forgotten his true purpose for being in the sleepy town.

'I forget, Rita. But what does it matter? We have found each other and that is all that matters now.'

Before she could speak again Zococa had bent his head down and placed his lips on hers. Without even knowing why, she found herself wrapping her arms around his neck tightly. He straightened up and took her full weight on his neck muscles before placing both his hands on her bottom. She seemed to have no idea that her feet were dangling twelve inches above the floor tiles as he made his way into the bedroom with her hanging on to him.

Carefully lowering her on to the bed, Zococa hovered over her, his head a few inches above her as their lips parted.

'You are Zococa, *señor*,' Rita sighed with her eyes closed as she savoured every second of the lingering kiss. 'Only the great Zococa could kiss like that. I felt as if I were floating on the very air itself.'

'I too felt myself floating, Rita. Floating into paradise.' Zococa smiled as he lay down beside her on the soft bedding.

'You are wonderful. Better than all the legends I have heard tell about you,' she continued to keep her eyes closed whilst raising her arms above her head and resting them on the sheets.

'I have never kissed anyone with lips such as yours,' Zococa lied as his fingers began to tease the silk bow of her bodice yoke apart. Her skin was dark and beaded with small droplets of perspiration. His lips found her soft throat and traced down between the firm breasts. She tasted good. So very good, he thought.

'You will be gentle with me, Zococa?'

'*Sí*, Rita. I will be gentle like the kitten.' Zococa peeled the white cotton apart and then rolled it down until her breasts were exposed to the moonlight that filtered into the room. Cupping one of the naturally tanned orbs in his hand, Zococa kissed the dark nipple tenderly.

Rita's entire body had shaken as if he had awoken some unknown emotion within her. Something that no other man had ever managed to locate previously.

'Zococa.' Her voice spoke his name softly as she felt his lips moving between her breasts from one nipple to the other. She felt breathless as a fire inside her was suddenly ignited.

'The bank!' Zococa said raising his head from her willing bosom.

'What?' Rita opened her eyes and stared at him.

'I now remember why I came to Broken Arrow, little one,' Zococa said sitting upright on the bed. 'I was here to see which of the banks in your little town might be worth robbing.'

'But we are making love.'

'*Sí*, Rita. Most passionate love.' Zococa stood and walked to the balcony and scooped his sombrero off the floor.

'Then why are you leaving, Zococa? We have not finished, have we?' She was now sitting upright watching the bandit placing his hat upon his head and staring down at the street below him.

'We have not even started, little angel.' Zococa grinned broadly as he went out on to the balcony and leaned on the iron railings.

'Then why do you leave?'

'Business. It is just business. For I am a villain. A terrible villain.' Zococa watched as she pulled her white bodice up over her naked chest. She ran to him.

Suddenly, the bandit hopped over the railing and dropped out of sight. Rita gasped and then found the bravery to look down from the balcony. The sight which met her eyes came as an unexpected shock.

Zococa was sitting astride his pinto stallion next to the massive silent Tahoka upon his own mount.

'Zococa,' she called down to him.

'I shall return, little one.'

Zococa thundered down the dark alley with his comrade at his side.

4

As Zococa led his Apache friend out of the fragrant alley on his impressive pinto stallion he raised both his eyebrows at the sight of the dozens of lathered-up horses filling the main street. The noise coming from within the saloon made it quite obvious to both riders where the masters of so many abandoned mounts were. Zococa eased back on his reins, stood in his stirrups and glanced through a small window of the busy building. He spotted the gleaming sheriff's star pinned to the cowhide vest of Tobius Randall, who was seated just below the window.

'Come look, my little rhinoceros.' Zococa indicated to his partner.

Tahoka steered his black gelding close to the wooden wall and looked down into the smoke filled saloon. He spotted the sheriff with his men and then started gesturing with his hands at the smiling bandit.

'Silence, Tahoka,' Zococa said, sitting back down in his saddle. 'I have a plan.'

Tahoka shook his head frantically as he watched the younger man starting to dismount. He waved both hands in front of the smiling face.

Zococa paused and sat back in his saddle.

'What?'

The gigantic Indian warrior began moving his fingers and hands carefully as he tried to make his concerns understood. For over a minute, Zococa watched and read his friend's silent words. As the Apache lowered his hands back to his reins he watched the face of the young Mexican.

'Are we to behave like old women? Are we to run and hide just because we have seen a tin star?' Zococa asked as he threw his leg over the neck of his horse and dropped to the ground beside the two mounts.

Tahoka touched the shoulder of Zococa. The younger man looked up and then smiled broadly.

'Do you never stop chattering, little one? You give me the headache. Nothing will happen to me because I am the great Zococa and I have a plan.'

The Indian looked heavenward. He knew that Zococa would do exactly what he wanted to do, however dangerous it was. That was the way the younger man did things. Yet Tahoka always felt it was his duty to try and dissuade Zococa from taking the risks he seemed unable to ignore.

Zococa stepped up on to the boardwalk and paused. He glanced back at the troubled warrior.

'Stop worrying. Soon we shall find a cantina and you can eat, my faithful one,' he said before moving towards the saloon doors. Unusually for Tahoka, he had no appetite.

The Horseshoe was a saloon like so many others in the countless towns that were dotted along the Texan side of the border. It had a bar which stretched from one end of the main room to the other with a gap for a carpeted staircase leading to the rooms on the upper floor landing which circled the main drinking area. A theatrical stage filled the western end of the huge room and even boasted a set of drapes imported from a Boston theatre. Each night the boards would be filled by dancing girls and singers who managed to keep their audience entertained in the hope of keeping them within the Horseshoe long enough for them to spend what little they had.

Yet there was one way in which the Horseshoe was unlike all those other saloons that graced the majority of Texan towns: it was owned by the town council of Broken Arrow and was run by and for the citizens of the town.

All the profits were ploughed back into the large imposing edifice, making it a place which was seldom empty and nearly always busy. The menfolk had long seen it as a duty for them to spend as much of their time and money in the four walls of the saloon as possible.

To most it was their second home, and to a few their only home. It had everything the average male customer could ever desire. Gaming-tables, subsidized liquor and females still on the shy side of thirty.

In fact, it was better than most men's real homes. For at least here they could drink until they dropped without anyone waving a disapproving digit at them.

Its fame had spread so widely that riders from south of the border regularly visited Broken Arrow just to go to the Horseshoe and enjoy its reasonably priced drinks and boisterous and cheap entertainment. On an average night of the week there were as many sombreros inside the large building as there were Stetsons.

Perhaps this was why nobody seemed to give Zococa a second look when he calmly entered the packed saloon and meandered to the busy bar. There were so many men of both Texan and Mexican origin within the noisy building that one more sombrero amid so many other sombreros and Stetsons was like a teardrop in the ocean.

Totally invisible.

'What'll it be, *señor?*' the barkeep who was closest to Zococa asked the handsome bandit.

'Tequila, *señor,*' Zococa replied placing a coin upon the damp surface of the bar.

'Coming up.' The man turned to the mirrored wall and began pouring the clear liquid into a small thimble glass.

Zococa nodded acceptance of the drink and stared at the three other bartenders who were just as busy as the man who had served him.

Sipping at the drink, Zococa watched with the intensity of an eagle on a high thermal. His eyes missed nothing as he stared from beneath the wide brim of his sombrero at the goings on all about him. The saloon was crowded to the point of being safer than a suit of armour.

Bodies could do little other than bump into one another as men made their way from one place to another inside the saloon. Zococa had not felt so utterly safe in years as he did standing against the long wooden bar.

No bullets could find him here, he thought.

Not in this mass of bodies.

Zococa knew it would be practically impossible for anyone to draw their gun out of its holster in such a heaving throng, even if he had been identified. Yet even though he was safe and totally unnoticed by all the liquor-soaked eyes which surrounded him, he knew he would not achieve his goal by remaining next to the bar.

He had to move to the other side of the room.

For there, in a corner at a table next to the elevated stage area, the glinting star on his distinctive vest, Tobius Randall was still seated.

Zococa placed two silver dollars on

the bar and pointed at a bottle of tequila with its seal unbroken behind the bartender.

'May I have the bottle, *señor*? I wish to give my friends a drink.'

'Sure enough, son.' The bartender smiled as he scooped up the coins and planted the bottle in Zococa's hands.

The bandit made his way carefully through the milling crowd slowly towards the lawman and what remained of his posse at the round card-table. They were all sitting beneath the small window, through which he could see the stony face of Tahoka in the alley. Zococa had been far closer to Randall over the past three nights than the sheriff could ever imagine. With a skill honed over the years, Zococa had deliberately taunted Randall and the posse until they had become totally confused and despondent.

But it had all been for a well-planned reason.

Zococa stood above the five seated men and smiled broadly as he placed the bottle of liquor on the table before them.

'I am a stranger in this town, *amigos*. May I join you with a bottle of tequila? I hate to drink alone and I also have to seek the wisdom of the sheriff.'

Randall ran a finger across his drooping moustache until his mouth was almost visible.

'I'm the sheriff, sonny. Drag up a chair and sit yourself down. Me and the boys will help you polish off this white lightning in exchange for me giving you some pearls of my wisdom.'

Zococa grinned, pulled a chair from beneath a sleeping drunken man and watched him hit the floor. The man seemed to be totally unaware of the incident as the bandit sat down between Randall and the nervous Wally Beer.

'This is most civilized and kind of you gentlemen to allow me to join you.' Zococa pushed his sombrero off his face.

'You bought the booze, son,' Jonas

Quaid said bluntly. 'We'll talk to anybody if'n they're buying the drinks.'

'My name's Sheriff Randall. What's your handle?' the sheriff asked as he pulled the cork from the bottle and poured measures of the strong liquor into the beer glasses of all the men around the table.

'I am Luis Santiago Rodrigo Vallencio, *señor*,' Zococa replied. He placed the thimble-glass under the neck of the bottle as the sheriff poured a full measure into it.

Randall seemed unable to grasp any of the name as it hit his befuddled brain.

'I'll never remember that mouthful, son.'

'Few can.' Zococa shrugged.

'That's a mighty big name,' Wally Beer observed, looking over his shoulder and out of the window at the moon, which hung in the night sky. For a fleeting moment he saw the face of Tahoka and blinked hard. When his

48

eyes focused again, the Indian had moved out of view.

'*Sí, amigo*. A very big name.' Zococa sipped at his drink as he tried to make out why the cowboy seemed so frightened. 'What are you looking at?'

'The moon,' Wally gulped. 'For a minute there I thought I seen a face but — '

'The moon is very bright,' Zococa interrupted quickly. 'It can play tricks on tired eyes.'

'It sure can when it's over my shoulder. That's a bad omen. I sure wish I had my lucky rabbit's foot on me tonight.' Wally Beer lifted his glass and downed the tequila in one go.

Zococa raised an eyebrow. 'You have the superstition?'

'Don't pay Wally no heed. He got kicked in the head once. He's plumb loco,' Sheriff Randall gruffed. 'What's your business in Broken Arrow, son?'

'I am here because of the banks, Sheriff.' Zococa continued sipping at his glass.

'You got some money to deposit?' Quaid asked.

'*Sí*. It is only a small amount, but I am not sure which of the banks is the safer to place my money in.' Zococa watched the faces before him. None seemed to be at all alarmed that a total stranger, fitting the description of a bandit they had chased for three nights, was interested in Broken Arrow's banks.

'You wanna know which is the safer of the two?' Quaid asked as he accepted another generous measure of the tequila into his beer glass.

'Exactly. I wish to know which bank is the safer one for me to put my meagre inheritance in.' Zococa smiled from behind the glass at his lips.

'Well, the First American bank is big but I figure the old Texas Mutual is probably the safer. Got walls in there four feet thick, I'm told.' Randall belched as the sheer power of the tequila made itself felt.

'Thank you, *amigo*. You have been

50

most helpful.' Zococa nodded and rose to his feet. He bowed to the assembled posse members before disappearing back into the crowd.

'That sure was a nice fellow,' Wally Beer said.

'Generous,' Jonas Quaid added.

'Salt of the earth.'

Tobius Randall poured the last of the contents of the tequila bottle into his empty glass and rubbed his aching head.

'He reminded me of someone but I'm damned if I can remember who.'

5

Evil, it is said, comes in many guises. Some are easily spotted by the keen-sighted, but there are other forms of evil which although appearing quite normal to the naïve, leave an acrid aroma in their wake.

The Double X Ranch was by far the biggest cattle spread along the border with Mexico. It boasted more than three thousand white-faced cattle and at least half as many longhorns, covering a range which had once comprised numerous smaller ranches. Now the Double X dominated all its competitors and, one by one, had managed to take control of more and more of the precious land.

In a mere handful of years it had become an empire. An empire owned by one mysterious man.

A man who was reputed to be unlike

any rancher the people of Broken Arrow had ever set eyes upon before. A man who ruled not only his cattle empire but his vast army of cowboys like a medieval tyrant.

He was known as Big John Denison, and that was about as much as most folks knew of the wide shouldered cattleman. For even after five years, Denison seldom came into the boisterous Broken Arrow. But his highly paid men were never far from the town or its legendary entertainment.

Denison had come into the lush grassy Texan plains with a massive herd of prime beef steers and a saddle-bag full of golden eagles.

It seemed, at first, as if Big John Denison was the saviour whom so many desperate people along the border had prayed long and hard for. A man who could bring prosperity back to the remote tract of Texan land.

Yet it did not take long for the rancher to make his mark around

Broken Arrow in a way most of the residents found worrying.

Seemingly not satisfied with his first land acquisition of a hundred thousand acres, Denison soon started to turn the screw on his neighbours until, one by one, they submitted. Ranch after ranch suddenly became part of the Double X. Like a gigantic leech, the Double X sucked the life-blood from more and more cattle ranches.

The owners of smaller ranches, who had managed to avoid being swallowed up by Denison's seemingly unlimited fortune and insatiable appetite, soon found their new neighbour a daunting figure who made his own rules and laws.

It was said he had used his money and power to control not only the law but the two banks within the bound-aries of Broken Arrow. Whatever the truth, John Denison seemed untouch-able and capable of doing what he pleased.

Soon after arriving in Broken Arrow,

Denison had angered the local population by refusing to hire anyone from Broken Arrow to work on the Double X. He preferred to use his own army of cowboys whom he had brought with him.

On first impressions it seemed that Big John Denison and his Double X Ranch was the most successful cattle spread in all of Texas. Yet it was an elaborate illusion, for, after five years, the herd had remained almost untouched. There were steers out on the vast range which all real cattlemen knew were far from their best and too old to take to market. They were allowed to graze the long sweet grass like pets. But no real rancher could afford to simply keep over 4,000 beef steers without driving some of them north every year. Big John Denison seemed able to do just that and still manage to get richer and more powerful with every passing day.

People had started to ask questions. How was Denison so successful?

He seemed never to send herds on trail drives, as all of the other ranchers were forced to do just to make ends meet.

Denison employed a vast army of men on his huge ranch who, it was becoming increasingly obvious, were not cowboys at all. Real hardworking cowboys did not ride around with expensive shooting rigs strapped to their thighs and loaded carbines beneath their saddles.

But these men did.

How could Denison afford to do this?

And why?

Questions were starting to be asked by the remaining ranchers who had noticed something brewing in the air in and around Broken Arrow.

Who exactly was this Big John Denison whom few had ever set eyes upon?

And where did he come from, and why? What was his secret?

It seemed as if they would never find

out anything more about the man who hid away in his large ranch house set in the centre of the Double X.

For there was no one in Broken Arrow who had the skill or cunning to match their curiosity concerning Big John Denison.

That might have remained the case, had not rancher Giles McGrath, owner of the small Cross G cattle spread recognized the two men who walked into the quiet cantina and headed for the darkest corner.

McGrath had almost finished his steak supper and was about to head back to his own ranch when he spied the handsome Mexican walking a few paces ahead of the massive Apache warrior across the tiled floor of the cantina.

McGrath began to smile.

'Zococa!' he muttered under his breath.

6

It had been a few years since their paths had crossed but no one ever forgot Zococa, even if they had only met for a few minutes. The unmistakable Tahoka was also one man that could not be confused with any other. He could make a grown man's blood freeze in his veins when he cast his emotionless hooded eyes in your direction.

Giles McGrath watched from his table beside the cantina's hot ovens and mopped up the remnants of his gravy with a chunk of freshly baked bread. He studied the pair in the opposite corner of the aromatic cantina with a knowing eye. McGrath knew from experience that it was never wise to approach these famous men too quickly.

They had to be given plenty of time to adjust to their surroundings. Time to look around and, with luck, recognize you first. For flamboyant as Zococa was, even he could get nervous when cornered in unfamiliar territory. Wily Giles McGrath knew this only too well, from experience.

Only when Zococa had settled down and studied every inch of the cantina with his keen eyes would it be wise to head in the direction of either man. McGrath knew that the handsome bandit was like a mother hen to the gigantic mute Indian. He also knew that Zococa would go without food himself rather than see Tahoka hungry.

There were many stories about the exploits of Zococa but Giles McGrath knew the truth behind those tall tales. The rancher had seen, at first hand, how the elegant bandit would risk his life for no financial reward to himself if he felt someone less able required his expertise.

Whatever inexplicable yet divine intervention had brought Zococa to Broken Arrow, McGrath was truly grateful. He alone knew the true worth of the ever-smiling man seated opposite his cluttered table.

McGrath lifted his coffee-cup to his lips and swilled the black beverage around his mouth before swallowing it. By this time the rancher had seen Zococa extinguish the flame of the candle set in the centre of the table at which he and Tahoka had sat down.

McGrath knew that Zococa had a habit of never sitting at a table with any kind of illumination. As the old rancher had heard the bandit say many times, light draws bullets as well as moths.

Zococa had struck a match and placed its flame to the tip of his long thin cigar as his eyes surveyed the cantina and its customers. Returning the silver cigar-case back into his jacket pocket covering his heart, Zococa stared through the smoke which trailed from his lips.

It did not take the bandit very long to recognize Giles McGrath.

The smoke drifted through the wide smile that covered Zococa's handsome face. He had removed his sombrero and hung it over the back of his hard high-backed chair before raising a finger to the watching rancher.

'Look, Tahoka. We have found an old friend.'

Hearing the friendly words, McGrath rose to his feet and placed a few coins on the napkin before walking across the quiet room toward the two notorious men.

'I see you boys are still alive and kicking, Zococa.' The older man smiled as he reached the table and stared down on the two men. It seemed odd to most people who did not know them or their story, that Tahoka and Zococa should be together at all. Giles McGrath knew why they were together and to him, it seemed right. He had often thought that Zococa's often foolish bravery might have cost the bandit his life long ago, had it not been for the silent Indian who managed to slow him down just enough to make the difference between life and death.

'Señor Giles. It is a pleasure to meet an old friend in a strange town such as this Broken Arrow.' Zococa waved at the cook to bring them a menu. 'Please join us for a little wine.'

McGrath pulled a chair away from the table and sat down. He nodded to Tahoka.

'You still riding with this young rooster, Tahoka?'

The Apache nodded.

'You're a mighty brave man.' The rancher smiled at the warrior.

'I forgot that your ranch was around this little town, Señor Giles.' Zococa shrugged. 'It is nice to have at least one wealthy friend.'

'I'm not as wealthy as I was,' McGrath admitted.

'When a man has friends, or at least one woman, he is wealthy, *amigo*.' Zococa flicked the ash carefully from the end of his cigar into the small ashtray set next to the candlestick.

'You look a tad red in the face, Zococa. What have you been planning?'

McGrath pushed the basket of bread towards the Indian whilst looking the Mexican straight in the eyes.

'Tell me, *amigo*,' Zococa started, 'do you happen to have any money in a bank in this town?'

'What little money I have is banked in the First American, Zococa. Why?'

The bandit raised both eyebrows.

'This is a great pity. We were going to rob the First American bank later tonight, but now it seems a little rude of us to even think about it.'

Tahoka chewed on his bread and started talking with his fingers and hands.

'What's Tahoka saying?' McGrath asked with a wry smile on his wrinkled face.

Zococa inhaled on his cigar deeply.

'Tahoka is begging your forgiveness, *amigo*. He had this plan to rob the bank and I had to go along with him.'

Tahoka stopped chewing and stared hard at his younger companion.

'Reckon that look on his face says a

damn sight more than even his fingers could ever do, Zococa.' Giles McGrath pulled out a pipe from his pocket and checked that its bowl was charged with tobacco before placing its stem between his teeth.

'I admit it was my idea, Señor Giles.' Zococa ran his thumbnail across the tip of a match and handed it to his old friend. He watched as the rancher lit his pipe.

The female cook had hair whiter than snow and a body wide enough to prove without doubt that she could rustle up a pretty good meal. Or at least eat one.

'I am very honoured to have the great Zococa in my humble cantina,' she said knowingly.

'Ah, the menu!' Zococa smiled, accepting the single piece of card from the woman. 'We shall have two large bowls of your chilli, much fried chicken and two bottles of your best wine, my pretty one.'

The female blushed.

'There is no need to flatter me. I have

no daughters, Zococa.'

'There might be snow on your head but there is still fire in your eyes, my lovely one,' Zococa grinned.

Giles McGrath shook his head.

'Don't you ever stop, son?'

'Why? She is handsome. A man would not feel the cold in her arms, Señor Giles.' Zococa glanced around the room instinctively before continuing: 'The food must be very good in this cantina, Tahoka.'

The Indian asked why with his hands.

'Is it not obvious? Never trust a skinny cook, my little one. For a skinny cook does not eat her own cooking. A fat cook eats the same food as she prepares for her customers. This cook is very wide and that means she is very good at her job.'

Tahoka finished off his bread just before the two bowls of chilli were placed before them.

'You boys seem pretty hungry. How come?' McGrath asked.

Zococa continued to smoke his cigar whilst Tahoka began consuming his chilli.

'I am not hungry, *amigo*. Not for food.'

'You looking for excitement and maybe some danger?' McGrath eyed the bandit as his teeth toyed with the stem of his pipe.

'*Sí, señor*. But mostly I seek money.' Zococa laughed. 'And the arms of a young woman to make the love with.'

'Are you up for hire?'

Zococa raised an eyebrow. 'You wish to hire the great Zococa? Who is it you wish me to kill, Señor Giles?'

'I don't want nobody killed.' McGrath leaned closer to the bandit and stared into the twinkling eyes. 'I need somebody to check out an *hombre* named Big John Denison. I need a man who is courageous.'

'You require Zococa!' The bandit nodded as he watched Tahoka looking up at them with a cautious stare carved in his stony features.

'Yep. I figure you might be the only one who can help me and the other small ranchers around Broken Arrow.'

Zococa glanced at Tahoka.

'Did I not tell you this town looked good for business, my little rhinoceros?'

Tahoka shook his head as he chewed. He started to talk with his hands frantically.

'This ain't no easy job, son,' McGrath said honestly. 'If'n you don't take it seriously, it might prove costly.'

Zococa rested a hand on Tahoka's sleeve. The huge Apache sighed heavily and stopped moving his hands. It was if he had reluctantly known that further objections were pointless.

'We shall do what has to be done,' Zococa said.

'Reckon we better go and meet up with the other ranchers and talk about the fee for your services.' Giles McGrath tapped the bowl of his pipe on the heel of his boot.

'No, Señor Giles. First we watch Tahoka eat whilst we drink two bottles of wine.' Zococa's eyes were fixed on the well-built female as she approached with the tray carrying the rest of their supper. In his heart he knew that robbing the bank was probably safer than getting involved with the intriguingly named Big John Denison, but there was a desperation in the face and voice of his old friend, Giles McGrath.

A desperation he could not ignore.

In his entire adult life, Zococa had never been able to turn down any genuine plea for assistance. The fact that McGrath had offered to pay for his help only made the inevitable decision more irresistible.

'Then we shall go meet with your *amigos*, Señor Giles.'

7

Big John Denison had paid out a small fortune having the ranch house, which stood in the centre of his Double X cattle empire, constructed. The imposing wooden three-storey structure would not have looked out of place in a large Eastern city, but standing in the vast grassy range, it appeared almost ludicrous. The bunkhouse was also far larger than any other on neighbouring spreads, but it had to be, just to accommodate the army of hired gunmen that Denison kept constantly around himself.

Yet neither structure could hold a candle to the massive edifice that towered over both of these. This was a building which oozed danger from every iron rivet.

Set a hundred yards behind the elegant ranch house, the immense structure seemed shrouded in a constant cloud of acrid smoke that had stained it with charred scars and choking fumes, yet none but the men who worked at the Double X had ever set eyes upon it.

If strangers had set eyes on the expertly constructed building with its sixty-foot-tall red-brick chimney-stack, which billowed black smoke and devilish red sparks over the heart of the cattle ranch, they might have guessed the truth.

But ever since Denison had first arrived in this remote land and purchased enough of its acreage to keep prying eyes well away from its very centre, no outsider had seen the strangely out-of-place building. The hired guns who masqueraded as cowboys had done and continued to do their job well. Nobody dared ride within the Double X boundaries.

The mounted army made sure of that.

For five long years the ever-growing

ranch had been protected from all intruders by Denison's loyal heavily armed cowboys. The secret of the Double X's mysterious wealth had been kept from all who might have been curious.

For all of that it was still a fragile secret. One which remained intact because of the high salaries Denison was willing and somehow able to pay.

Big John Denison stood like an unyielding oak-tree upon his screened veranda watching the long trail road, bathed in moonlight, that carved its way through the swaying grass and countless steers. The rancher screwed his eyes up and studied the dust coming off the hoofs of five of his riders as it drifted on the warm evening air.

If ever a man deserved a nickname, it was he. For in his tall Cuban-heeled boots he stood nearly seven feet in height. There was not a glimmer of emotion upon the tanned brutal face which watched the five familiar riders who were aiming their cutting horses at the huge house.

The big man did not move a muscle until the men stopped their mounts and tied their reins around the hitching pole beneath his elevated position on the screened porch of the veranda.

Brad Cutter led his associates up the stone steps. He opened the screen door and they all entered the illuminated area.

'We done seen that posse riding around again, Big John,' Cutter informed the statuesque figure.

'They still chasing that bandit and the redskin?' The words seemed to fall from the lips of Denison almost without his mouth moving.

'They still reckon that Zococa character is around Broken Arrow someplace,' Cutter added.

'He must have his eye on one of the banks,' another of the men named Sam Potter added.

Denison turned his head and glared at the dust-caked men. He showed no signs of emotion as he spoke.

'You figure them bandits are actually in the vicinity?'

'Reckon so, Big John.'

'He's been leading the sheriff and his idiots a merry dance.'

Denison walked towards the five men. They parted and allowed him to pass between them. Each of the men watched the huge hands of their boss. They were clenched so hard that the veins stood proud from the tanned skin.

'That could be awkward,' Denison muttered in a low growl.

'Zococa ain't gonna hinder us none, Big John,' Cutter said.

'I've heard of this Mexican. He's trouble. The one thing I cannot afford right now is trouble, boys.' Denison snorted. 'I've spent too much money and too much time for it all to go belly-up.'

Brad Cutter stepped away from the four other gunmen and edged close to the right arm of the rancher. He could see the eyes flash in his direction.

'There ain't no way he can stop us, Big John.'

'But if'n he does rob one of the banks, and takes his money to another town,' Denison paused for a moment before continuing his sentence, 'folks might just figure out what we've been doing here.'

'I don't get it?' Potter said.

Brad Cutter turned to his confused comrade.

'Think about it, Sam. If Zococa steals money from one of the banks and tries to spend it someplace where they ain't as dumb as the Broken Arrow bankers, folks might just put two and two together.'

'I still reckon Zococa can't do us no harm,' Sam Potter insisted.

'Not if he's dead,' Denison whispered.

'What ya mean?'

'The only certain way to keep Zococa out of my business is to kill him.' Denison turned his head and looked down on the men who had been with him since they had first arrived in this land. Men who had shared in the illegal profits that their well-oiled enterprise had yielded.

Brad Cutter rubbed his chin. 'That might prove a tad harder to do than say, Big John.'

Big John Denison looked at each of the five men in turn. They were just a fraction of his army of hired gunslingers and each no better or worse than the next. Each knew only two things; how to take orders and how to kill.

'Twenty of you boys ought to be able to find two riders, Brad,' Denison said confidently. 'A fancy Dan Mex and a stinking redskin. Find them and kill them. You all know what'll happen if'n you don't.'

'Finding is one thing but actually getting the better of that pair is another, Big John.' Cutter rubbed the sweat off his face with his bandanna.

'Are you boys scared?' Denison cast his eyes across each of the five faces before him.

Faces which were frozen with fear as they stood in the lantern-light.

'Nope. We ain't scared, Big John,' Cutter replied.

'We is a mite troubled though,' Potter shrugged.

'Troubled?' Denison boomed. 'As troubled as you'll be if the Texas Rangers come snooping in here and find out what we're doing in that building?'

'If'n you put it that way, I guess you're right.' Sam Potter looked down at his feet.

'There are men in that bunkhouse who can shoot the wings off a fly, boys,' Denison said confidently. 'You can all out-shoot any *hombre* who has the grit to stand up against you. I don't see any way that bandit and his tame Indian can stand up against them odds.'

Cutter swallowed hard. 'Reckon you're right, Big John.'

Potter nodded hard. 'Yep. Damn right.'

'Tomorrow I'm sending my own

Double X posse out after that damn Mex and his Indian pal. If Sheriff Randall and his bunch of no-hopers can't catch that bandit, you boys can. The reward will be a sort of bonus for you. I want this blasted Zococa character dead. There ain't no other way.' Denison walked past the men and entered his huge house.

The five men felt the dust hitting their faces as the door slammed behind him. They knew that when tomorrow came, they would have to do exactly as Big John Denison ordered.

Brad Cutter led the men toward the bunkhouse. He had heard many stories about the famed Zococa, none of which filled him with any confidence that it would be possible to execute Big John's orders successfully.

'I don't like this, Brad,' Sam Potter muttered.

'I'd rather face Zococa than Big John any day, Sam.'

8

Chill Weaver had once owned the Texas Mutual Bank but for over two years he had been little more than a highly paid puppet. His name and title were still embossed in gold leaf upon the mahogany door, but within the wood-panelled office, Weaver was utterly powerless. A mere figurehead.

Only two men in the vicinity of Broken Arrow knew the true details of this strange agreement.

One was Weaver himself and the other was the reclusive rancher known as Big John Denison.

Weaver poured himself another large whiskey and downed it in one swallow as he brooded from behind the desk he had used for nearly two decades. He stared through the iron bars which protected the solitary window of his office, at the darkness that still loomed outside.

Even the soft light of the moon failed to comfort the despondent banker. For Chill Weaver knew that he had become little more than another of Denison's hired hands. It was a situation that gnawed at his innards like a cancer and no amount of hard liquor seemed able to take the troubled worry off his shoulders.

For he knew why Denison had moved into this land. Of all the assorted souls along the Texas border, Weaver was the one man who knew the truth. The men who rode for the rancher were privy to parts of the overall story, but it was Chill Weaver who had worked it all out in his calculating banker's brain.

The reality of his position did not sit well with the elderly man, yet Weaver could see no way out of the financial cesspit he had willingly allowed himself to fall into. As is the nature of all bankers, he had a merciless streak in him, but knew he had been totally outwitted by John Denison. Perhaps it was rough justice for all the mortgages he had so happily foreclosed on over the years. Maybe there was a higher judge who had decreed it was Chill Weaver's turn to taste the bitter fruits of torment and helplessness.

Whatever the reason, Weaver thought he had struck paydirt when two years earlier he had been visited in the dead of night by the man known as Big John. With hindsight he knew that he had made the biggest mistake of his life in agreeing to the seemingly generous proposals of the rancher. Weaver had been lured, as most men in his position would have been, by the golden eagles which were spread out on his desk that night.

For some reason, Denison had paid more than three times the true value of the Texas Mutual. A sum which in itself was enough to make the banker more than willing to do anything to keep the huge man happy.

As with most men in his questionable profession, Chill Weaver had thought he had the better of the tall man. When Denison had asked him to stay on and run the bank for him, it seemed his opinion of the rancher was correct.

Too much money and too few brains.

Denison's request that they keep the transaction between themselves was another thing which made Weaver believe he was dealing with a half-witted person. Who in their right mind would spend so much money and want to keep it a secret?

Weaver toyed with his glass and imagined he could still see the gleaming freshly minted golden eagles spread out on the ink blotter of his desk. Weaver had almost drooled at the sight of so much money: money, which unlike all the rest in his vault, belonged not to his depositors, but to him. He had raked it towards him like a riverboat gambler and willingly agreed to everything the rancher had asked of him.

Greed could twist even the straightest of men. Weaver knew in his heart that he had never been too far away from submitting to his own darker nature. Denison had found his weakness and used it to his own cunning advantage.

Weaver shook his head and poured yet another large whiskey from the nearly empty bottle. His entire body shook at the memory of his signing the papers which Denison had so conveniently placed before him.

He had sold his soul that dark night, and he knew it.

Weaver swallowed the drink and rubbed his sweating face dry with a handkerchief. That had been the beginning of the end for the one-time highly respected banker. Now he was merely someone who jumped when his strings were pulled. He knew what was happening to the money within the vaults of the Texas Mutual, but could not do anything about it.

Not without the entire town finding out. To go to the authorities would mean ruin not only for Denison but himself. It was a price he was not willing to pay.

So he continued to be the rancher's puppet.

Big John Denison certainly knew exactly how and when to pull those strings. He had been controlling every aspect of the Texas Mutual Bank ever since that fateful night. A night which Weaver knew had been the end of an illustrious career.

From that fateful clandestine meeting, Weaver did exactly as he was told, knowing that to go against a man such as Big John Denison would be tantamount to committing suicide, both professionally and literally.

The banker finished the contents of the whiskey bottle and somehow managed to get to his feet. His head was filled with a million reasons to cut and run, but his courage had long deserted him.

Now all that was left was to wallow in self-pity. Each night he would drink himself into the pitiful wretch he had become. It was the coward's way. It was his way.

He staggered to the window and reached up to the cord hanging from the blind.

The tapping on the window pane caused him to look down. He focused on the familiar figure of Giles McGrath, who stood in the alley with two other men veiled in shadows.

'Can I talk with you, Chill?' McGrath's voice asked through the window-glass.

For a moment Chill Weaver's liquor-soaked brain wondered what he ought to do. In all the days he had been in banking, he had never been robbed. Even recognizing the smiling face of McGrath would have not allowed the banker of old to allow these men inside his beloved bank. Yet Weaver was not the man he had once been. This was no longer really his bank at all. He remembered that this was now John Denison's property, whatever everyone in Broken Arrow thought.

'Sure, Giles. Hold on a tad.' Weaver

stumbled drunkenly to the rear door of his office, slid the bolt across, then turned its handle and pulled it open.

9

The three men walked from out of the shadows of the alley, into the gloomy office illuminated by a single oil lamp upon the desk. Zococa and the silent Tahoka made their way to the far wall whilst Giles McGrath remained close to the man he had long thought of as a friend. The sound of the door being closed and then bolted again behind them echoed around the wooden walls of the banker's office. They turned to face the obviously distressed Weaver.

'Sorry to disturb you, Chill. But it's kinda important,' McGrath said, watching the drunken banker leaning on the door. In all the years that the cattle rancher had known Weaver, he had never seen him like this.

Weaver walked unsteadily towards his desk and rested his hip on its edge. He ran his fingers through his limp hair and then cleared his throat.

'No trouble at all, Giles. What's on your mind?'

'We need your help,' McGrath said. He saw the banker's face focus on the two men who had accompanied him into the office.

'I'm listening. Carry on.' Weaver gestured with his hands, his eyes never leaving the handsome bandit or the Apache warrior who were toying with the large cigar-box next to the ink-blotter.

'You know that I and what's left of the ranchers around here have been having a tough time of it lately,' McGrath began. 'We have been holding secret meetings trying to get to the bottom of a few things.'

Weaver looked at the stout rancher.

'I don't understand.'

'We figure that something's happening out there on the Double X, Chill.' Giles McGrath sighed heavily.

Weaver felt a cold shiver racing up his spine at the mere mention of Denison's cattle spread. He knew exactly what was happening out there amid the thousands of acres of grazing land.

'What you getting at, Giles?'

'We want to know if you'll join us at the meeting that we are having tonight at the Bar T?' McGrath moved closer to the banker who was now visibly sweating.

Weaver looked straight into the face of the rancher.

'I don't know why you want me at your secret meeting, Giles. I'm not even a rancher. I don't understand what you think is happening on the Double X ranch, but whatever it is, it ain't nobody's business except Denison's. Nope, I think I ought to keep out of this.'

Zococa made a quick gesture with his fingers. His silent comment made the Apache nod in agreement.

'We need an upstanding member of the community to make sure we do everything above board and legal.' McGrath rested a hand on the shoulder of the banker. He could feel it shaking.

'Nope. I don't want no part of it.' Chill Weaver stood and glared at Zococa and his companion. 'And who are these two men, Giles? Gunslingers?'

'I think you are a little afraid of my quiet friend and myself, *amigo*.' Zococa smiled and lifted the lid of the large cigar-box resting next to the empty whiskey bottle. The sight of so many expensive cigars made the bandit pick one up and run it beneath his nose.

'Who are these two men, Giles?' Weaver asked again balancing against the edge of his desk as he watched Zococa pulling out a handful of cigars from the wooden box.

'We are ruthless villains, *señor*. Desperados.' Zococa grinned as he handed one of the cigars to Tahoka and then placed the rest of the long Havanas into his silver cigar-case.

Before Weaver could respond, McGrath spoke.

'Ignore his joking, Chill. These boys

are the salt of the earth. I'd trust them with my life.'

'Who is he?' Weaver pointed a shaking finger at Zococa who was sliding the silver case back inside his jacket.

'He's just a friend. He's on our side, Chill.' McGrath gave Zococa a glance which begged the bandit to behave. 'That's all that counts.'

'I heard tell that Zococa the bandit is in the area.' Weaver seemed to straighten as he heard his own words dripping from his mouth.

'Zococa the handsome bandit, *señor*,' Zococa corrected the banker.

'Zococa is on our side, Chill,' McGrath insisted.

'I don't take sides, Giles. I think you and the rest of your secret society are headed for trouble. There are laws against vigilante gangs taking the law into their own hands.' The banker walked unsteadily back to the rear door of his office and released its bolt. 'I reckon you had all better go.'

'This is a very nice little bank, Tahoka.' Zococa nodded to his huge friend. 'I can smell the money.'

Tahoka nodded.

'Is that your last word, Chill?' McGrath asked the worried man.

'It is. I reckon you had better get going, Giles. And take this pair of bandits with you.' The banker felt a sudden guilt overwhelming him. Weaver knew he had a lot to lose if the truth of his involvement with Big John Denison ever became common knowledge.

'But this Denison is up to something, Chill. Everyone in and around Broken Arrow knows it. He ain't sold a steer in the five years he's been on his land and yet he's richer than the rest of us ranchers all put together.' McGrath tried vainly to make the banker look him in the eyes.

Weaver pulled the door open.

'Leave now. Take your so-called friends with you. I want none of it. All I can see is trouble headed your way if you continue on your present course, Giles.'

Giles McGrath shook his head and strode back into the alley with Tahoka close on his heels. Neither man looked back as they walked to their waiting mounts.

Zococa was more deliberate in his leaving of the office. He paused next to the banker and used his index finger to lift the flabby chin until Weaver was forced to look directly into his eyes.

'I think you are troubled by something, my friend. Something which eats at you and makes you seek sanctuary in the bottom of a whiskey bottle.'

'How dare you talk to me that way?' Chill Weaver flustered angrily.

'I dare, señor.' Zococa smiled and slowly walked out into the dark shadows of the alley. Before the door closed, he glanced over his shoulder at the trembling man. 'I am the great Zococa and am always willing to dare and tell the truth when my friends are in trouble.'

10

As the morning sun began to creep across the mountain town of San Pueblo it was obvious that few of the whitewashed stone dwellings perched upon its steep cliffs had escaped the wrath of Orlando Fernandez and his two followers.

Blood seemed to be everywhere. Red and inescapable. It stained the walls of the buildings and covered the stone road that wound its way from the very summit down to the valley below. If ever a place looked as if it had been visited by the Devil himself, it was San Pueblo.

The smell of gunsmoke hung on the fresh crisp air whilst the continuous muffled sobbing echoed around the buildings. Yet the carnage had not ended. It would continue until someone within the boundaries of the high mountain settlement told Fernandez what he wanted to know or the last of the people were dead. The Mexican colonel cared little either way.

It had gotten out of hand and Fernandez knew it. He had tried to control his men and also his temper but failed miserably on both counts. The night had been a long one filled with torture and merciless killings. Yet for all the bloodshed, the people of this remote community refused to reveal anything about their famed son.

They remained blindly loyal to Zococa. Far more loyal than the bandit would have ever wanted them to be. Zococa had many faults but letting innocent people pay with their very lives, just to protect him, was not one of them.

The Mexican colonel had started with the men of San Pueblo and pistol-whipped as many as his two soldiers could find. That had failed to make them talk. Then he had decided to use his sabre on the tightlipped peasants.

This too had failed.

Then Fernandez had lined up women against a wall and given them five minutes to talk before he allowed Remo and Concisco to fire their rifles.

But the women had also died without opening their mouths.

Orlando Fernandez had never experienced such blind loyalty before in his entire military career. The streets were littered with the proof of their love of the bandit Zococa. It confused the soldier more than he would dare admit.

It also enraged him.

He would not allow these peasants to defy him any longer. They would now have to be taught just how low he was willing to stoop to get the information he desired.

As the morning light of a new day drifted over the terrible carnage he had created, Fernandez decided to try one last ploy to get the remaining people of San Pueblo to talk.

They would have one final chance to tell him where their beloved 'hero' had gone.

Carlos Concisco and Jose Remo did as instructed and gathered up as many children and infants as they could locate amid the blood and guts of the high mountain town. The two soldiers dragged their small prisoners through the streets until they reached the cantina. They had kicked and pistol-whipped their young captives with each step they took to ensure that they had a audience for Fernandez's grand finale.

They did.

Tying the children to the hitching pole outside the cantina, the two soldiers stepped back and allowed Fernandez to begin his ultimate atrocity.

Wielding his bloodstained sabre above his head, the Mexican colonel strode up and down before his tethered, sobbing prey.

As the morning light filtered through the branches of the tall trees and displayed every savage killing he and his men had committed during the hours of darkness, Fernandez slowly began to notice the score of bleeding adults gathering all around him.

Turning to face them, Fernandez raised his sabre until the sunlight gleamed off its honed edge. He knew that he had now gained their total attention. Now that he was preparing to kill their children, they were suddenly afraid.

'I give you one last chance,' Fernandez shouted at the faces of the surviving men and women of San Pueblo. 'Tell me where Zococa has gone and I will spare these children. Say nothing and I shall chop off their heads, one by one. The choice is yours.'

A wailing moan seemed to fill the small square around the Emperor's three agents. Slowly the sound grew until it was a deafening crescendo of begging parents and grandparents pleading for mercy.

But there would be no mercy.

Not until Orlando Fernandez had the information he desired. The tall Mexican moved to the side of the youngest child and rested the blade of his sabre on the nape of its neck. His eyes flashed at the crowd as he slowly raised the lethal weapon up into the air again.

'Tell me now!' Fernandez screamed at the crowd.

A woman crawled away from the rest of the sobbing people with her hands clawing at the air. Her clothing was already stained with her own blood which bore evidence to the fact she had already tasted the bitter fruits of personal torture.

'I will tell you, *señor*. I will tell you what you want to know,' she cried. 'Please do not harm my little baby.'

Fernandez kept his sword hovering until she was at his feet. 'Tell me, woman. Where has Zococa gone? Where has the filthy bandit gone?'

'To the town of Broken Arrow, *señor*,' she said as her tears fell on to his boots.

'Broken Arrow? Where is this place?' Fernandez asked.

'Over the border.' She added breathlessly, 'Less than a day's ride, due north.'

Fernandez nodded and walked away from the woman toward his two watching men. He tossed the sabre into the hands of Remo.

'What do you wish me to do, *señor*?' the smiling soldier asked as he ran his thumb along the blade.

'Cut the head off the man we mistook for Zococa yesterday,' Fernandez replied.

'But why? He is already dead.' Jose Remo rubbed his whiskers as he stared up into the face of the grimfaced colonel.

'Because if we cannot find the real Zococa, we shall require something to take back to the Emperor, Jose.' Fernandez spat at the ground. 'Put it in a bag and tie it to the saddle of the pinto stallion.'

'Do you think we will not find the

real Zococa?' Concisco asked.

'I think we will ride to this Broken Arrow, Carlos.' Fernandez sighed, staring at the blood and bodies which surrounded them. 'I hope the people there will be less loyal to Zococa than these fools.'

'But what if they are not?' Remo glanced at Fernandez.

'Then we will have our work cut out for us, *amigo*.'

'But why do we need the head of the other man, *amigo*?' Carlos Concisco asked wearily.

'The Emperor will bestow much gold for the head of Zococa, Carlos.' Fernandez's eyes narrowed. 'Whatever happens, I intend getting that gold.'

11

Giles McGrath rode slightly ahead of Zococa and Tahoka as they headed into the heart of the Cross G Ranch. The night had proved fruitless for the elderly rancher and he knew it. He had tried vainly to arouse the interest of the other ranchers into doing something to halt Big John Denison's total take-over of the rich cattle land.

But for all the fiery talk that came from the mouths of McGrath's fellow cattlemen, there was no fury in their bellies to match their passionate words.

Zococa reined in his stallion and dismounted outside the impressive ranch house. He allowed his horse to drink from the overflowing trough and watched McGrath tying his reins around the hitching pole next to him.

'You have many friends, *amigo*,' Zococa said to the troubled rancher.

Giles McGrath removed his Stetson and shook his head.

'I have never seen such a bunch of yellow-bellied bastards before, Zococa.'

Zococa removed his saddle from his mount as Tahoka slid from the black gelding beside them.

'Your words are very harsh, Señor Giles. These are men with families. Men with the pretty wife and children are not as willing as some to risk getting shot.'

McGrath looked at him. He knew the words were true.

'These men are suffering as badly as I am but they just won't make a stand and try and see what this Denison character is up to, Zococa.'

Tahoka moved to the older man and rested a hand on his shoulder. He talked with the fingers of his free hand and watched as the young Mexican nodded.

'Tahoka say it is time we all slept.'

McGrath shrugged. 'You boys can stay in the house with me. I got plenty of empty rooms.'

Zococa rested his saddle on top of the hitching pole and walked towards the disheartened man.

'Where is your family, *amigo*? Your wife and sons?'

'All gone, Zococa,' came the chilling reply.

'Dead?' Zococa reluctantly asked.

'Yep. The fever got them all a couple of years back.' McGrath beat his hat against his leg and turned towards the house.

As Zococa and his Apache companion followed the rancher, the bandit suddenly noticed the silence which filled the area.

'Where are your cowboys, Señor Giles?'

'Only got three full-time hands working on the Cross G nowadays, Zococa,' McGrath replied. 'They're off tending what's left of my herd of longhorns.'

Zococa stepped up on to the raised porch and paused as his two friends entered the silent house. He knew there was a curse on this land. He could sense it.

Yet he had faced and defeated such things many times before and knew he could do so again.

'Señor Giles?'

'What, Zococa?'

'I have a plan.'

12

They were an awesome sight as they thundered across the flat grassy range toward the still half-asleep town. Broken Arrow had never witnessed this many heavily armed riders entering its narrow streets before. The open mouths of the early risers bore testament to that. The townspeople had never seen the tall rider at the head of the riders before either.

Big John Denison led his small army astride an eighteen-hand buckskin with all the confidence of a seasoned army officer. It seemed his desire to ensure Zococa was captured and killed had been the one thing capable of bringing the reclusive rancher off his Double X cattle empire.

It was Denison who drew the reins up to his chest first and stopped his lathered-up mount outside the sheriff's office. The men all stopped around him, like a massive shield.

'Randall!' Denison shouted at the open doorway.

There was no spoken reply as the sheriff ambled out of his office and on to the boardwalk. Tobius Randall sipped from a tin cup before squaring up to the fearsome figure of Denison.

'Reckon you must be Big John Denison,' Randall said, casting his eyes around the more recognizable figures of the Double X riders. 'What can I do for you?'

'Deputize me and my men!' Denison demanded.

Randall lowered his cup and stepped closer to the snorting nostrils of the big buckskin mount. He then looked at its master long and hard.

'You all wanna be deputies? Why?'

'Somebody has gotta get this Zococa character,' came the solid reply.

'I don't understand, Mr Denison.'

'It's simple, Sheriff. Just hand out the tin stars and say the words and we'll go and find this bandit.' Denison seemed to be unable to say an entire sentence without snarling.

'But I don't need no extra deputies.'

'Make us deputies, Randall!' Denison screamed.

Randall tossed the remnants of his beverage away and felt a cold shiver trace up his spine. He had never seen the owner of the Double X before but had heard countless stories about the man. It appeared that they were all true.

'But I've been heading a posse out every night for days now, Denison. We ain't managed to get within a shooting-distance of the wily young fox. What makes you think you and your boys can do any better?' Randall felt uneasy as his eyes watched the big man dismounting.

Denison stepped up on to the boardwalk and towered over the lawman.

'Because my boys ain't barbers and newspaper editors. My boys are paid to be able to use their weapons.'

Sheriff Randall nodded. He had no idea why, but it seemed wise to agree with a man of such incredible proportions as Denison. He led the ranch owner into his office and pulled down a cardboard box filled with dozens of stars.

'Help yourself, Denison,' Randall said, feeling every argument evaporating from within his heaving chest as he stood beside the gigantic rancher.

Denison did.

He scooped the box up off the desk and marched back out into the early-morning light. He threw the stars into the hands of his score of riders.

Randall poked his head around the doorframe and stared at the broad-shouldered man who seemed content to distribute the shining badges.

'How come you are so fired-up about this bandit?' he heard himself ask the smouldering rancher.

There was a long pause before Denison threw the empty box away and turned to face the lawman.

'I'm a law-abiding man, Sheriff. When I hear that there's a ruthless bandit roaming around the vicinity, I gets kinda angry. When I'm angry, I gotta do something to help my less capable friends. I want to kill Zococa and help you and the citizens of Broken Arrow.'

Randall felt sweat pouring down his face. He had locked horns with many men before but none who made him feel as inadequate as this rancher.

'I make you all temporary deputies,' Randall said, waving his hand at the twenty or more riders before him.

Denison stepped down off the boardwalk, grabbed the reins of the buckskin mount and set off along the street with his entourage of riders behind him.

He was headed for the Texas Mutual Bank.

When he reached the building the rancher tied his reins to a wooden porch-upright. He then stepped up into the shade and stared at the locked doors and the golden lettering painted on to the glass window-panes.

Brad Cutter dropped off his horse and jumped up next to the silent Denison.

'What you doing, Big John?'

'I'm waiting to talk with Chill Weaver, Brad,' came the snapping response.

'I thought we was getting on this Zococa's tail, boss?'

'We will. I got me some business to do first,' Denison announced sternly looking at his line of riders all wearing their newly acquired deputy stars. 'I think you ought to take most of the boys out and start tracking that Mexican.'

'But where do we start?' Cutter pushed his Stetson up off his face and looked into the eyes of the brooding man.

'The river is the key, Brad,' Denison replied. 'I hear he uses the river border to slip in and out of Texas.'

Cutter's jaw dropped.

'The river goes on for ever, Big John. We'll never find him if we have to try to cover the entire length of it.'

Denison shook his head in frustration and grabbed both shoulders of the smaller man with his gloved hands.

'Are you dumb or just plain stupid? There are only a few places where a rider can cross the river safely. You check them out and when you find some tracks, follow them.'

Cutter swallowed hard and returned to his horse. Holding on to the saddle horn he hopped up until his left boot found the stirrup and then threw his right leg across the broad Texas saddle.

Denison pointed at Sam Potter.

'You stay with me.'

'Sure thing, Big John,' Potter said rubbing his nose along his shirt-sleeve.

The rest of the force turned their mounts and galloped down the long street after Brad Cutter. They had their orders and they would obey them. For, however lethal these gunmen were, they feared incurring the wrath of the tall rancher.

Denison heard the green door-blind being raised behind him and turned to face the man he had controlled for five years. The door was unbolted and then pulled open.

'Mr Denison?' Weaver's voice could not conceal the shock at seeing the infamous rancher in daylight.

'We gotta talk, Weaver,' Denison growled before entering the bank.

13

With grim foreboding, Chill Weaver slid the black metal bolt across, securing the front door of the Texas Mutual. He followed the towering figure of Big John Denison through the empty bank, and into his quiet office. Weaver's stunned staff watched silently from behind their various counter-windows at the strange sight of their employer actually taking orders from a man they had never set eyes upon before.

The older man felt an unease he had seldom experienced before as their footsteps echoed around the cool interior of the building whilst he followed the gleaming spurs.

The rancher never usually came to Broken Arrow during the hours of daylight, preferring the protection of darkness to shield him from the curious eyes of the town's citizens. Something had forced the hermit crab out from its protective shell.

But what?

Why had Denison come to the Texas Mutual now? Weaver kept asking himself. What had happened to make this creature of habit alter his routine?

Making his way cautiously to his desk, Weaver felt the grim-faced rancher's eyes follow him across the office as he walked. It was like being studied by a circling eagle as it swooped lower and lower toward its chosen prey.

'What in tarnation's wrong, Big John?' Chill Weaver reluctantly asked the huge man. 'What's brought you into Broken Arrow in daylight?'

'Zococa!' The name was spat out of Denison's mouth as if it were poison.

Chill Weaver felt the power of the tall man before him.

'Why are you so worried about this particular bandit, Big John? He ain't nothing special.'

'I happen to know a little bit about this Zococa critter,' the rancher growled angrily. He clenched his fists. 'He's slippery, Weaver. He'll get in here if he's a mind to do so. I've had me and some of my men deputized and we'll have to catch that Mexican before he gets a chance to break into here. Because if Zococa does rob the Texas Mutual, he's sure to find out what we've been up to for the last couple of years.'

Weaver sank down into his comfortable chair.

'What we've been up to? You own this bank, not me. You're the one who has orchestrated everything illegal around here. Don't try to rope me into your mess.'

'You're in this as deep as me, old man.' Denison's gloved finger prodded Weaver's chest with every word that left the big man's lips. 'You've sat back and clawed your share of the profits. If Zococa busts in here and steals any of them special golden eagles I've been minting on the Double X, everything will blow up in our faces.'

'But how? We've been carefully

distributing the special coins all over the state for two years now. There's no way they could ever be traced back to us, Big John,' Weaver retorted.

'Think, man,' Denison screamed. 'When we've been unloading our counterfeit eagles for genuine ones, right across Texas, it has been done carefully and to a precise plan. I've made sure that none of our fake golden eagles has been seen within a hundred miles of here so that nobody could locate us or our mint. If Zococa steals even just a few of them coins, he could spend them around here. That would bring the Treasury boys down on our backs. How long do you figure it would take for them to find us out?'

Chill Weaver felt his heart sink.

'Zococa was here last night. Standing exactly where you are, Big John.'

The unexpected statement stunned the rancher. Denison stared in disbelief at his unwilling accomplice.

'Zococa was in here? In your office? What the hell do you mean?'

'McGrath of the Cross G brought him here,' Chill Weaver explained. 'They even brought the Indian with them.'

'Why?' Denison dragged the top drawer of the banker's desk open and hauled out the whiskey bottle he knew would be there.

'McGrath wanted to try and enlist me into his small group of ranchers who have been getting kinda het up about you and the financial success you're enjoying.'

Denison pulled the cork from the neck of the bottle and took a long drink. Then he gritted his teeth.

'But what the hell was Zococa and his tame Indian doing with him?'

'Beats me. I reckon McGrath must have hired them as gunslingers.' Weaver knew his reply did not sit well with his partner in crime.

'So Zococa is in cahoots with McGrath.' Denison slammed the bottle down on top of the ink blotter and wiped his mouth along the back of his gloved hand. 'I'll get my boys rounded up and pay the Cross G a visit.'

Chill Weaver rose to his feet. 'What you intending to do?'

Big John Denison tapped the deputy's star on his coat and smiled. It was a gruesome, chilling smile.

'I'm not going to do nothing personally, Weaver. The law will take care of Zococa and the bastard who's harbouring him. I'll have them all swinging on the end of Double X ropes before sundown.'

The banker watched the rancher walking out of his office. Weaver had never heard Denison laughing before. It was a frightening sound that the banker prayed he would never hear again.

14

Felix Snape slid the honed edge of the straight razor across the throat of his nervous customer with a hand that showed all the signs of the previous evening's over-indulgence in the busy Horseshoe. As a crimson bead of blood began to trace down the neck of the sweating man seated in the barber's chair, Snape shook his head and stepped back to stare out into the bright street.

'For Christ sake, Felix,' the bleeding man said as he forced the reclining chair upright and glared at the damage in the steamed-up mirror. 'I didn't come here for you to carve me up.'

Snape rested his hand against the door frame and looked at the blood on the blade.

'I'm sorry, Hank.'

'What the hell is up with you today?'

Snape tossed the razor into a washbasin and then exhaled heavily as he too tried to figure out what was making him so nervous.

'I had me a late night with Tobius and the rest of the posse, Hank.' Snape moved back to his customer and with a wet towel tended the damage he had done.

'I've seen you hung-over too many times to fall for that crap, Felix.' Hank's voice came from beneath the thick towel. 'What's really wrong with you?'

Snape pressed his thumb against the inch-long gash and then locked eyes with the customer reflected in the mirror. The effects of the liquor-sodden night before were indeed still affecting him but that was not why Snape had been in a cold sweat for more than an hour. For it had been a mere hour earlier that he had watched the twenty riders with the awesome figure who could have only been the infamous Big John Denison, passing his barber shop.

It had been a sight which had chilled

him to his very core because the face of the broad-shouldered rancher was one he remembered from his less than wholesome past.

The problem was, the face did not match the name.

Denison had glanced straight through the window of the small barber-shop at the slightly built Snape, as he led his men down the main street of the sleepy town. To the cattleman Snape was just another barber with too much oil holding down his centre-parted hair.

Yet Snape's memory was far sharper.

It had been a long time ago and several hundred miles north of Broken Arrow, but Felix Snape never forgot a single face that he had ever shaved during his entire career wielding his trusty straight razors. They were all branded into his brain, warts and all.

The face of Big John Denison was now much older, but still memorable to those who had crossed his path and lived to regret it. There were few faces that had remained carved into the barber's brain with such total clarity but Denison's was one which had done just that. Yet if all the stories he had heard over the intervening years were true, Denison should no longer exist.

'You're still shaking, Felix. How come?' the bleeding patron asked as he watched the reflection in the mirror of the barber's troubled face draining of colour.

There was a long silence before the barber managed to get the words to clear his dry throat.

'Tell me, Hank. Do you happen to believe in ghosts, by any chance?'

'Ghosts?'

★　★　★

Sheriff Tobius Randall dropped his coffee-cup on to his cluttered desk as Felix Snape burst through his open doorway and rushed up to the wide desk.

'Tobius! Tobius!'

'Hold up, Felix. Calm down, ya damn fool. I almost had me a heart attack,' Randall shouted, studying the dark beverage as it dripped off his paperwork and soaked into the lap of his dust-caked pants. He was thankful that the coffee was no longer hot. 'What the hell is eating at you, Felix?'

'Big John Denison!' Snape said. He inhaled quickly and tried to steady himself.

'Yep. He was here a while back. So what?'

'Did ya see his face, Tobius?'

'Reckon so. Leastways, I saw as much as most folks considering he wears that Stetson pulled down over his eyes.' The sheriff frowned thoughtfully.

'I seen his face clear as I see yours. And I tell you something, it ain't belonging to that name.'

Randall grabbed at a Wanted poster and dabbed his lap.

'What the hell are you jabbering about, Felix?'

The barber leaned over the desk and

stared hard into the older man's eyes.

'His name ain't Denison.'

Randall ran a thumb across his chin. 'Not Denison, you say?'

Felix Snape nodded hard.

'I know him from a long ways back, Tobius. He ain't no respectable rancher at all. He's a road agent and worse.'

'You gotta be mistaken.'

'I ain't making no mistake, Sheriff. Anyone who ever met up with that particular *hombre* in the past has good reason to recall him and his deeds.' Snape rolled up one of his sleeves and showed the melted skin which surrounded a deep cruel scar. This was no ordinary wound but the physical remnant of a branding.

'Good grief!' Randall exclaimed in horror. 'Who did that to you, Felix?'

'The critter who calls himself Big John Denison done this to me. I can still remember hearing him laughing as I passed out in agony.'

'What's his real name?'

'John Clinton was his handle back

then,' Snape said in a brooding tone.

'He wanted?'

'I reckon he must be.'

Sheriff Randall dragged a large drawer open, lifted a pile of old Wanted posters out from its cobwebbed belly and dropped them down before him. Without saying another word, the lawman slowly began to thumb his way through each of the browning sheets of paper with a care he had never before used.

'The thing is, Tobius,' Snape added nervously, 'John Clinton was said to have been killed more than eight years back.'

'Then he's a mighty healthy-looking ghost,' Randall observed. 'And I deputized the varmint.'

15

Giles McGrath could hear the sound of hoofs somewhere off in the distance as he rose sleepily from his well-worn couch and gazed at the wall-clock hanging over the chimney mantel. It was almost noon and he had slept for nearly four hours.

The last thing he could recall before succumbing to the tiredness only a man who has remained awake throughout the hours of darkness can understand, was the famed Mexican bandit eating breakfast with him.

Zococa had not eaten that much but kept pushing food before his gigantic Indian friend. Yet he had talked. Constantly and eagerly until the elderly rancher could no longer listen.

McGrath rubbed his sore eyes again, and moved to the clock and opened its glass cover before searching for the key inside one of his vest pockets. He had lost count of exactly how many times he had wound this old clock up over the years and had long forgotten exactly why he did so. It had become a habit, a ritual serving little or no purpose out on the vast Texas ranges. Perhaps it was the ticking that echoed around the room that made him do so. Like the heart of an old friend beating.

Just as he was about to raise the worn brass key and insert it into the face of the clock, the rancher's attention was once again drawn to the sound of approaching horses.

McGrath moved away from the clock, still holding on to the key, and gazed curiously through the netscreened door. At first he could see only dust rising from the almost flat land beyond his boundary fencepoles. Then his tired eyes caught sight of the riders themselves. There was a score of them.

The elderly rancher was about to call out over his shoulder to his two guests when he noticed that both the black gelding and Zococa's magnificent pinto stallion were no longer tied up alongside his own mount.

Zococa had boasted earlier that he had a plan. Giles McGrath remembered that much from his conversation with the ever-smiling Mexican. Whatever that plan was, he must have taken his faithful Apache companion with him to execute it, McGrath surmised. With the sound of horses' hoofs growing louder, he wished the bandit had delayed his departure.

Suddenly there was a dryness in the throat of the watching cattleman as he focused on the line of horsemen who were closing in on his ranch house.

Who were they?

What did they want here?

Even as the questions flashed through his tired brain, he knew the answers deep in his craw. It could only be one man at the head of such an army, he thought. Denison! No one else could afford to employ that many men.

Finally Big John Denison had come out from his well-protected ranch and was paying him a visit.

But why?

Had Denison somehow got wind of what he and the other ranchers had been discussing the previous night? If so, McGrath could not think who had betrayed his trust.

Stepping out into the mid-morning sunshine, the rancher paused on his porch and waited for the riders to reach him. He knew he ought to be afraid, although he felt that he had not done anything to warrant being so. There was something carved into the faces of the determined horsemen as they reined in their mounts which told McGrath this was no sociable call.

Dust swirled around the Cross G courtyard as the riders all lined up around their stony-faced boss.

As the choking dust finally settled the old rancher noticed that these riders were packing more weaponry than he had ever witnessed anyone honest carrying. Whatever these riders were, McGrath knew they were not cowboys.

Although he did not announce himself, it was obvious that the lead rider, who held his horse's head in check with gloved hands gripped tightly around his reins, had to be the mysterious Denison.

McGrath stepped closer to the edge of his wooden porch and looked up into the hard face. It was a sight that chilled him to the bone. If ever there was evil etched in a human face, this was it, he thought.

'You must be Big John Denison.' The owner of the Cross G spoke nervously.

Denison nodded. 'You ain't as dumb as you look, McGrath.'

McGrath felt a cold shiver tracing his spine. It was as if the words he had just heard were dipped in the venom of a striking sidewinder.

'What you want on the Cross G? State your business.'

Denison glanced to either side of him

and at the heavily armed riders he had led to this place. Every one of them seemed to be waiting for the slightest of signals from their leader. Just waiting to be given the word to act.

'Reckon this old critter thinks Big John and his Double X rannies are stupid or something, boys,' Denison growled. 'Maybe we ought to teach the bastard a lesson.'

There was a noise from the riders. It did not contain words, but was a sound that seemed to echo off the wooden buildings around the Cross G court-yard.

Giles McGrath dropped his hands to waist level and then realized he was not wearing his gunbelt. He glanced over his shoulder into the house and could see his weapons in their holsters, resting on the arm of the long couch. He had never been an expert with the guns but felt helpless knowing that they were just out of reach.

A thousand things raced through the mind of the elderly rancher as he slowly turned his head back to face the line of horsemen.

Where were Zococa and Tahoka?

What did Denison want here and why did he ride with so many men if he was simply what he claimed to be?

There were no answers though. Only cold sweat that ran down his face and back.

Giles McGrath toyed with the clock-key in his hands and somehow managed to muster enough courage to step to the very edge of his porch and gaze into the cold lifeless eyes of Denison. Maybe he could bluff his way out of this situation, he thought. McGrath had always managed to do so in the past but he had never faced anything as daunting as this before.

'I told you to state your business, Mr Denison.'

Denison almost grinned.

'You got grit, old man. I'll give you that.'

'I'm a busy man. Tell me what's gnawing at your innards and then vamoose.' McGrath was somehow managing almost to convince himself that he was not afraid of these men although he could hear the sound of gun and rifle hammers being cocked to both sides of the emotionless Denison.

'You hired that Mexican cut-throat Zococa, I'm told.'

The words froze the old rancher in his tracks. How could Denison know that unless someone he trusted had spilled the beans?

'I don't understand.'

Denison pulled back his jacket and displayed the deputy's star he wore on his vest.

'We're the law. All legal and everything, McGrath. We are looking for Zococa and his heathen pal. When we find them we'll hang 'em high. Seems to me, anyone who is in league with them outlaws deserves to have his neck stretched too. What do you reckon, old man?'

For the first time since the unexpected arrival of the Double X riders on his Cross G ranch, Giles McGrath found himself stepping backwards.

'Who you bin talking with, Denison?'

'The same coward that you blabbed to.'

'Weaver?'

'That's the spineless dude,' Denison confirmed.

The blazing morning sun seemed to dance across the barrels of the Winchester repeating rifles as they were trained on him. McGrath suddenly knew what it felt like to be a human target. His eyes flashed from one grinning horseman to the next trying to see a glimmer of mercy in one of their faces.

There was none.

'Hold up there!' McGrath yelled at the top of his voice. 'What you varmints intending to do?'

Big John Denison nodded his head and raised a gloved hand to his men.

It was the signal they had all been waiting for. The rifles all began spewing out their lethal lead. Bullets ripped through the body of Giles McGrath from all directions until it was torn to shreds. Within half a heartbeat the entire porch of the ranch house was awash with putrid gunsmoke.

And blood.

16

The riders thundered steadily upward towards the only cover within five square miles. Zococa dragged his reins hard to his chest and halted the lathered-up pinto under the canopy of a dozen broad-leaved trees. The shade was a welcome relief to the bandit as he pushed his black sombrero off his damp brow. Although the afternoon sun was beginning to wane, it was still ferocious to anyone or thing out in the open.

Standing in his stirrups Zococa waited for Tahoka to catch up with him. He surveyed the scenery with the eyes of a man who knew his very survival rested on his ability to spot trouble long before it actually occurred.

When the silent Apache stopped his horse beside his more flamboyant friend, Tahoka also studied the land around them. They were deep in the heart of the Double X and it was becoming more and more obvious that this place was no ordinary ranch like its smaller neighbours. This place seemed to offer little in the way of normality. Aged steers were scattered across the rolling plains simply eating their fill.

To their surprise, the two bandits had not seen one cowboy since they had first entered this secretive place. Where were the heavily armed men that Denison was reputed to employ?

The first thing Zococa had noticed when they had ridden up to the boundaries of the Double X, was the barbed-wire fencing which completely surrounded it.

Even Zococa knew that to find any barbed-wire fencing on Texan soil was rare. Ranchers here tended to share the rolling range, not cut out chunks of it for their own use. Yet the Double X seemed to require penning in for some unknown reason. It appeared that this man-made barrier was not designed to keep the longhorns in, but rather, keep

Denison's fellow ranchers out.

Or at least prevent their prying eyes from learning the truth of what lay hidden within the heart of the massive ranch.

Yet a mere razor-sharp barbed-wire fence could not obstruct Zococa and Tahoka. Both riders had cut their way through it and headed straight for the hills where Giles McGrath and his fellow ranchers had told them they would find the ranch-house nucleus of Denison's empire.

Now they were close to discovering what truth.

'Did you not think it was odd that the Double X ranch is completely fenced, little one?' Zococa asked as he stared ahead of them. 'I mean, it is like a graveyard here, is it not? Why do they need a fence at all?'

Tahoka attempted to reply but his hands and fingers were no match for the quicksilver tongue of the Mexican.

'I have often wondered why there are tall walls around cemeteries,' Zococa added. 'I think those who are inside cannot get out and those outside do not wish to get in.'

The huge Indian thought about the statement and was about to respond when the smiling bandit beside him started talking once again.

'This is most interesting, my little one,' Zococa said, squinting at the hill before them with an intensity rare for the bandit. 'Do you not think it is so?'

Tahoka began to wave his hands around in a vain attempt to reply.

'Quiet. Do not make the noise, Tahoka. I cannot think if you chatter like an old woman.' Zococa pointed and then watched his companion staring out at the hills.

Tahoka nodded.

'You see the smoke?' Zococa asked as he sat down again in his saddle.

The Apache warrior nodded once more.

'What would make so much smoke in the middle of a cattle ranch, *amigo*?'

Tahoka began to raise his hands once more.

'You are chattering again, my little rhinoceros. How can you be so annoying? Come. We will take a look.' Zococa tapped his spurs into the flesh of the noble stallion and rode straight at the summit of the hill with Tahoka on his trail.

The two riders stopped their mounts on the very top of the hill and stared down at the Double X complex below. What met their eyes did not seem to fit in with any cattle ranch either of them had ever visited before. The strangeness was only matched by the smell that lingered over the entire area.

The acrid smoke billowing from the large chimney on one of the buildings seemed to swirl around the courtyard like a miniature twister. Even from their high vantage point, both riders could still taste the smoke.

'What is that they are cooking, *amigo?*' Zococa said spitting at the ground trying vainly to rid his mouth of the taste. 'It is not very appealing.'

Tahoka agreed and indicated that they should leave by pointing back over his shoulder.

'Not yet. First we have to take a closer look inside that smelly building,' Zococa said bluntly. 'Anything that smells that bad must be worth a lot of money, I think.'

Tahoka urged his mount on down the steep slope after the tail of the galloping pinto. Even though every sinew of his soul told him it was foolhardy and probably dangerous to do so, he followed his friend.

As always, Tahoka silently followed.

17

Hired gunfighters, Sam Potter and Bob Brown had considered themselves lucky when Big John Denison had decided to leave them at the heavily wooded border-crossing waiting to see if Zococa might dare to cross the shallow river once more to taunt the seemingly useless Sheriff Tobius Randall and his ramshackle posse.

To them it seemed that this might be the easiest day's pay they had ever earned, that they had drawn the long straws, because they doubted if the Mexican bandit and his Apache companion would even bother to show up during the hours of daylight.

As far as Potter and Brown could tell from the multitude of tall stories which surrounded Zococa, he was too cunning to risk his neck without the cover of darkness to protect him. But they did not mind wasting an entire day by the river if it meant that Denison was somewhere else. He was a hard taskmaster and no mistake.

Potter and Brown had settled down to an easy day of eating jerky and smoking. As long as the grub and tobacco held out, they would be happy.

For more than five hours Sam Potter and Bob Brown had been undisturbed as they rested beneath the branches of a large tree twenty feet from the water's edge. They had laughed at the fact that their boss was leading the rest of the Double X men in an almost fanatical search for the elusive bandit whilst they just lazed around.

Neither man could understand why the usually calm and collected Big John Denison had suddenly become so irrational. They had never seen the tall owner of the Double X showing the slightest hint of fear before about anything, yet his reaction to the news that Zococa was somewhere in or around Broken Arrow gave all the appearances of a man who was frightened.

Very frightened.

Before either man could talk more about how lucky they were to have been saved the pain of riding to who knew where, trailing their leader, something interrupted their talking.

Suddenly both men's attention was caught by something in the woodland directly across the river. A flock of birds rose noisily into the blue sky and squawked overhead as they instinctively fled.

Sam Potter was the first to rise on to one knee. He lifted his Winchester off the ground. He knew something had frightened the birds and, whatever it was, it was heading their way.

Bob Brown dragged himself up from the ground and slowly paced across to the saddle of his quiet mount. He withdrew his rifle from its long scabbard.

'What ya figure it is?' Brown asked as

he sucked the last of the smoke from his cigarette.

Potter rose to his full height and cranked the mechanism of his repeating rifle but said nothing. His eyes and ears were trying to work out what was moving through the undergrowth on the Mexican side of the river.

The sound of snapping underwood seemed to echo all around the two gunfighters as the pair drew closer to one another. Whatever it was, it was moving over the dry ground opposite, straight towards them.

'Could it be Zococa, Sam?' Brown asked again.

Potter raised the Winchester to his hip and trained the long barrel in the direction of the sound. He had never been a man who was afraid to use his arsenal of weaponry and had done so on numerous occasions, but there was something about this which made him doubt his own abilities.

'Is it Zococa?' Brown asked again.

'Could be, Bob. I ain't ruling it out.'

'You figured that he would only cross the border after sundown, Sam,' Brown said as he, too, warily trained his weapon on the bushes and trees across the river.

'That's what I said, OK.' Potter stepped away from the shadows and gritted his teeth. 'Might be someone else.'

Brown shadowed his pal.

'That must be it. Gotta be some other varmint.'

Both men stood at the water's edge and watched the bushes being rustled until finally the riders broke cover and emerged into the sunlight.

For what seemed an eternity the Double X men stared at the three riders who were holding their mounts in check silently. It was obvious that they were Mexican. The rider who headed the small group was tall and elegant and sat proudly in his saddle watching the gunfighters. His two comrades seemed less well bred and sophisticated.

Sam Potter focused on the pinto stallion whose reins were tethered to the saddle horn of the lead rider.

'The pinto!'

Brown nodded and spat out his cigarette.

'Zococa rides a pinto.'

'That's gotta be him.'

'How come he ain't riding it, Sam?'

'That don't worry me none.' Potter raised his rifle until its wooden stock was nestled into his shoulder, then he stared down the long shining barrel at the three stationary horsemen.

Orlando Fernandez steadied his horse and called out over the glistening water:

'What is wrong, *amigos*?'

Brown swallowed hard and felt his rifle shaking in his sweating hands.

'He don't look like no bandit, Sam.'

Potter ignored his partner and stepped into the slow-moving river to respond to the Mexican.

'We know who you are. Now get them hands high or we'll blast you into the next world.'

Fernandez knew a little English but not enough to grasp the entire sense of the frantic yellings which had come at him from the mouth of the nervous rifleman.

'What did he say, Colonel?' Remo asked, nudging his horse next to the pinto.

'I am not sure, Jose,' Fernandez admitted.

Carlos Concisco stealthily drew one of his pistols from its holster and cleared his throat.

'I think these men are outlaws.'

'Are they trying to rob us?' Remo shrugged.

For a moment the trio of ruthless Mexicans studied Potter and Brown and the deadly Winchesters which were aimed at them. They had ridden long and hard to reach this place in their search for the elusive Zococa, and were in no mood to waste time arguing with a couple of shouting gringos.

Sam Potter fired a high warning shot

over the heads of the three riders.

'I ain't joshing, boys. Get them hands up in the air.'

Fernandez glanced to either side of him at his companions. His voice was low and steady.

'Kill them!'

Sam Potter and Bob Brown had barely time to blink when they saw the gunsmoke coming from the barrels of the three riders' handguns. Before the ear-splitting sound had reached their ears, both men felt the thudding impact of lethal lead hitting them off their high-heeled boots. Instinctively, the two Double X men squeezed their Winchester triggers as their backs hit the hard ground.

In was a futile gesture to even attempt to get back up on to their feet, yet both men attempted to do so as Fernandez led his men across the shallow flowing water. With every stride their horses took in the cool river, their masters fired their guns straight at their prostrate targets.

By the time the horses' hoofs were on dry ground again, the gunshots' job had been done.

It would have been impossible to count the bullet holes which filled both Potter's and Brown's bodies but neither Orlando Fernandez nor his two men paused long enough to try.

They reloaded their guns and then continued deep into the Texan landscape. For them, the real fight was yet to come.

18

Tobius Randall had been staring at the crumpled Wanted poster for more than an hour. The image that stared up from the browning paper was grainy and not the best he had seen that day, but there seemed no mistaking the eyes of John Clinton. They were the same eyes that had borne down on him from beneath the Stetson when Big John Denison had demanded he and his entire entourage be made deputies. In all the years he had worn the sheriff's star, Randall had never been so confused or worried.

The rumours that had surrounded the goings-on within the boundaries of the Double X ranch were now flooding over the ageing lawman. He had listened to the other ranchers in the neighbouring valleys and now he knew that they were well-founded. Felix Snape had been correct when he had told him that Denison was once a ruthless outlaw.

Randall stared at the poster again and thought about the words which claimed this hideous creature was worth $1,000 dead or alive. He knew it was a bounty he would never be capable of collecting, not with his part-time collection of deputies. They were mere ranch hands and newspapermen and the like. Not the sort to face up to someone like Denison, let alone when he was surrounded by a score of well-armed men.

Randall was still pondering what to do next when the hapless Wally Beer shuffled into the sheriff's office rubbing his nose along the back of his sleeve.

'Howdy, Toby.'

'Wally,' Randall acknowledged.

'What ya got there?'

'Who do you reckon this is, Wally?' the sheriff asked the bumbling deputy, lifting the Wanted poster off the pile.

Wally Beer accepted the crumbling poster and stared at it.

'Ugly critter.'

Randall rolled his eyes. 'Does that look like John Denison to you, Wally?'

Beer shook his head, then nodded. He had caught sight of the tall rancher when he had ridden up to the sheriff's office and demanded that he and his men be deputized.

'Yeah, now you come to mention it.'

'Only the name is different,' Randall sighed. 'Just like Felix said it would be.'

Wally Beer scratched his head. 'It is?'

'It says John Clinton on the poster, doesn't it?' Randall pointed.

Beer seemed none the wiser. 'I'll have to take your word for that, Sheriff.'

Tobius Randall stood up and moved to the window. He had forgotten that his superstitious friend could not even read his own name let alone anything else.

'I'm sorry, Wally. I forgot.'

'What does this mean, Toby?' Beer asked while placing the Wanted poster back on top of the cluttered desk. 'How can one man have two handles?'

'He can't. Leastways, not legally.' Sheriff Randall rubbed his chin and watched the deceptively quiet street. 'I had Felix send off a wire and the answer came back a few minutes ago. John Clinton was reported killed in a bank hold-up.'

Wally Beer sat down thoughtfully. He was still confused about the fact that a dead man could still be alive.

'The critter who came here earlier looked alive to me, but I've been wrong about such things before,' Beer muttered as his mind drifted. 'I was starting to think that Zococa bandit was a ghost. It's all too much for me to figure, Toby.'

'Zococa is real enough.'

'Maybe we could use Zococa's help to handle Big John, Sheriff,' Wally Beer said staring at his troubled friend. 'I heard a few stories around the saloon that old Giles McGrath has hired him.'

Randall raised an eyebrow. 'McGrath has hired Zococa?'

'Yep. That's the story.'

'If it's true, maybe that young Mex ain't as bad as he's painted out to be.'

'So Clinton is said to be dead and yet — '

'Kinda convenient for our Big John Denison to appear shortly after John Clinton dies, huh?' Randall interrupted.

'You figure that Denison is really a crook?'

'Seems that way. No honest rancher could throw money around the way he has.'

Wally glanced sideways. 'What's he doing around Broken Arrow? There must be bigger towns for someone like him to hang out in. I wonder why he came to Broken Arrow.'

'That's what I'd like to know, Wally.'

'Something else is troubling you,' Beer observed.

'Yep. You're right.'

'What is it then?'

'I deputized him and all his hired help, Wally,' Randall said coldly. 'I've given them a licence to kill anything and everything that stands in their way.'

Wally Beer fumbled in his vest pockets until he located a moulting rabbit's foot. He pulled it out and then started to look at it with an intensity which was unique to himself.

'What's that, Wally?'

'My lucky rabbit's foot. Why?' Beer replied.

'You got a spare one of those that I can borrow?'

Wally Beer scratched his head again. He was confused and it showed.

'Are things really that bad, Sheriff?'

Tobius Randall shook his lowered head. He was about to reply when he spotted the line of dusty riders returning and heading towards the Horseshoe Saloon.

Even at the length of the street, the Double X men were an unmistakable bunch.

'Where do you reckon Zococa might be, Wally?'

'The Cross G?'

'Saddle our horses. We better pay McGrath a visit.'

19

The afternoon sun had fallen from the heavens and was now casting long shadows across the Double X ranch as it hovered above the rolling hills that surrounded the ranch house and array of outbuildings. There was only another hour of sunlight remaining as Zococa and Tahoka quickly dismounted and tied their reins around a wooden upright at the rear of the ranch house. They had not seen one living soul on their approach to the massive foundry that continued billowing acrid black smoke from its enormous chimney-stack.

There seemed to be no one in or around the massive Double X compound as the pair of bandits tried to get an idea of what they had ridden into.

There was an air of danger here. The

air was choking and tainted by the smoke which continuously billowed out of the towering chimney. Neither man had ever seen its like before and could not even imagine what it was for.

'I do not like this my little one. Sometimes a place can be too empty of people.' Zococa coughed as he rested his back against the whitewashed wall. His eyes darted everywhere within their field of view. 'At least the sun is now going down, giving us the cloak of night as protection.'

Then they decided to move. Both men gripped their pistols and ran along the spine of the ranch house and across the barren ground between it and the strange edifice.

'Look, Tahoka. A door,' Zococa said pointing with the barrel of his silver-plated gun.

Tahoka touched his partner's arm and then Zococa's lips. It was obvious to the Mexican that his friend had seen something which concerned him.

'What is it?' Zococa whispered.

Tahoka pointed at the door in the side of the large building. It was being opened. A flash of light traced across the flat ground ahead of them. It was now half open and casting a strange reddish light out onto the sand.

The shadow of a man could be seen stretching out across the courtyard as he walked out of the building. Tahoka made a quick gesture with the fingers of his left hand before holstering his pistol.

'*Sí*, little one.' Zococa nodded to his friend. The large Apache ran silently with a speed that defied his enormous size towards the doorway. There was a swiftness and accuracy in the hands of Tahoka when he grabbed the man around the neck and brought him down on to the ground. Although the man tried to call out, it was impossible. Tahoka smothered the man's face before hitting the jaw with a powerful clenched fist.

When Zococa reached the spot his mute friend had rendered the man senseless with an expertise few others could equal.

'I hope you did not kill him, *amigo*,' Zococa remarked, while looking around the open doorway into the building. He knelt down beside his friend. 'It is very hot inside there. Why should it be so?'

The Indian watched as Zococa placed a hand upon the wall of the building and then pulled it away quickly.

'The wall, it is hot! What is this place?'

Tahoka shrugged and looked around the area for more of Denison's men. He could not see any but felt no easier. He had followed his young companion into many treacherous situations but none like this.

Zococa studied the unconscious man. He was not dressed in a fashion that was recognizable to the bandit. He was practically naked with the exception of a full-length protective leather apron covering trousers cut off at the knee. His boots were reinforced with metal toecaps.

'What is this man wearing?' Zococa whispered into the ear of his friend. 'I think he must be a blacksmith or something, my little elephant.'

Tahoka shrugged again.

'We must enter this devilish place,' Zococa said, rising to his feet and cocking the hammer of his gun back until it fully locked.

The Apache drew his own gun once more and then touched the sleeve of his partner. Both men glanced into each other's eyes before heading inside the building. They knew that this was probably the most dangerous of the places that they had ever ventured into. For this was the unknown.

Unlike anywhere either of them had ever gone before.

How many other oddly clad men might there be within the walls of this building, the two bandits wondered as the heat burned into their faces and the blinding light stopped them in their tracks.

Then they heard raised voices and the unmistakable sound of guns being readied for action.

Instinctively, Zococa pushed his huge partner sideways to the ground before throwing himself in the opposite direction. Bullets came from two different directions and tore up the ground between them.

The Mexican bandit gazed around at what was giving him cover. He was at the base of some huge brick structure. The heat from it felt like a hundred camp-fires. With his back to the bright light, Zococa was able to see again. He held his right hand up and signalled Tahoka to remain exactly where he was while he himself cautiously looked around for whoever it was firing at them.

Zococa fired. He had no idea where his targets were but knew he had to try to draw their bullets in his direction, away from Tahoka, who had less cover.

A bullet skimmed the edge of the brickwork beside his left shoulder. He then heard another gun being cocked ten yards to the right.

There were two of them, he thought. Just two.

Zococa fired his gun again quickly and then drew back behind the brick wall. More bullets bounced off the ground beside his legs, sending cement-dust into the air.

Opening the chamber of his pistol, Zococa withdrew the two spent cartridges and replaced them with new bullets from his gunbelt. Then he snapped the chamber shut and cocked his hammer again.

More bullets bounced off the wall at his side, covering him in red dust.

He knew roughly where their adversaries were and how many bullets they had fired. Taking a deep breath, Zococa bit his lip and rolled out from his place of protection.

Without hesitating for even a second, Zococa began to fan the hammer of his trusty pistol. The blinding light from the massive smelters obscured his vision and the shimmering heat-haze made everything within the huge building appear to be swimming before his eyes.

But even obscured by an ocean of burning air, Zococa could see the flashes of gunfire coming from the pistols of the two men. He had started with only six bullets and had made every single one of them count.

Zococa continued fanning his gun hammer until it fell on empty chambers.

The muffled screams had told Zococa that his aim had once more been true.

Slowly the bandit rose to his feet, clutching his smoking silver gun in his left hand. Sweat poured down his face as the heat from the furnace blistered the side of his face.

'Get up, Tahoka. I have defeated our enemies,' Zococa said whilst walking up to a huge metal box full of gleaming golden coins.

'Look, *amigo*. Have you ever seen so many coins?' Zococa remarked. He reloaded his gun and slid it into its black leather holster.

The huge Apache warrior lifted a handful of the coins and studied them. Zococa took one, and placed it between his teeth and tested it.

Zococa raised an eyebrow.

'Now I understand.'

20

Darkness spread swiftly across the lush Texan range as the two lawmen rode from Broken Arrow toward the once prosperous Cross G ranch. Yet even as they approached both horsemen sensed that something was not quite right. Sheriff Randall had never before ridden into the courtyard of the Cross G ranch after sundown without there being lanterns illuminating his way towards the ranch house. Teasing the reins back he slowed his bay mare until it finally stopped. Wally Beer drew level with the law officer and then held his own horse in check.

'This don't feel right, Wally,' Randall remarked, drawing his Colt .45 and cocking its hammer. 'Giles McGrath always keeps a welcome light burning for his wranglers and the like.'

'Maybe he forgot tonight,' Beer

whispered drily.

'McGrath ain't the sort to forget anything,' Randall said looking all around them for even a hint of human life. 'I got me a feeling our pal Denison paid the Cross G a visit earlier today.'

'But why?'

'Maybe he heard the same gossip about Zococa that we did.'

'So?'

'Denison had a bee in his bonnet when he came visiting me this afternoon,' Randall recalled. 'He seemed to be real troubled by the news that Zococa was in this neck of the woods. That's why he demanded I deputize him and his gang.'

'But why would he come here, Sheriff?'

'To find out more about Zococa or maybe just teach old man McGrath a lesson. Who knows?' Tobius Randall rubbed his mouth. It was dry.

'I don't like this one bit.'

'Me neither, Wally.'

The nervous deputy twisted his head

around and looked up at the haunting moon.

'I told ya that it ain't lucky to have the moon over your shoulder, Sheriff. This is the Devil's work, I tell ya.'

'Quit jabbering, Wally,' Randall snapped angrily. 'I got me a feeling that whatever has happened around here it's the work of real living breathing men.'

'McGrath!' Beer called out several times at the top of his voice. 'You there, McGrath?'

There was no reply.

'Maybe he's gone someplace,' Beer suggested.

'Maybe. Maybe not,' the sheriff said. Then he noticed the rancher's horse still tied up to the hitching rail. 'If he went anywhere, he went on foot. Knowing Giles McGrath, I kinda doubt that.'

Both riders slowly dismounted and led their mounts cautiously forward, using the light of the moon as their only guide.

The sight which met their eyes upon the ranch house porch caused both men to hesitate for a moment. Even in the pale gleam of moonlight there was no mistaking the hideous bullet-ridden remains of Giles McGrath as he lay where he had fallen hours earlier.

'You see that, Wally?'

'I see something. What'n hell is it?'

'A body.'

'Is that old man McGrath, Sheriff?' Wally Beer asked trying not to look down at the gut-turning vision.

Randall swallowed hard, stepped up on to the porch and knelt down. Striking a match, the lawman gritted his teeth as he focused on the unholy carnage.

'Yep,' Randall drawled before the flame of his match blew out in the gentle evening breeze. 'It's old Giles all right.'

Then suddenly behind them they heard the sound of horses' galloping towards the courtyard. Both lawmen rushed into the centre of the wide yard to get a better view.

'I see two of them, Sheriff,' Wally Beer said trying to pull his pistol from its holster with fingers that seemed unable to respond.

Tobius Randall squinted out across the flat range at the pair of horsemen heading quickly towards them. Even in the shimmering moonlight he could make out that one of the riders was atop a pinto whilst the other had long hair flapping in the spectral light of the moon.

'Who is it? Can ya make them out?' Beer's voice seemed to have reached an even higher pitch than usual.

'That looks like a Mexican and an Indian to me, Wally,' Randall replied hesitantly.

'Zococa?'

'Reckon so.'

Wally Beer dropped his gun on to the ground. 'That's just dandy, Toby. Just dandy.'

Both of the Broken Arrow lawmen stood motionless as Zococa and Tahoka drew in their reins and halted their mounts.

For a moment the bandit simply sat in his saddle staring down at Randall and Beer. His face was etched with confusion.

'What are you doing here, *amigos*?' Zococa asked as he carefully dismounted before the men whom he had led a merry chase for more than three days.

'You must be Zococa,' Randall said.

'*Sí*. I am called Zococa,' the bandit admitted. 'But you have not answered my question.'

'You don't know anything about this?' Sheriff Randall pointed the barrel of his Colt in the direction of the moonlit porch.

Zococa dropped his reins to the ground and strode towards the porch. It was a scene he had neither wanted nor anticipated. For once he was as silent as his mute travelling companion. The handsome bandit took a deep breath before turning to face the sheriff.

'Who did this, *señor*?'

Randall released the hammer on his gun with his thumb and returned it to its holster. For some reason the sheriff instinctively knew he had no need of its deadly power with these two strange riders.

'You had nothing to do with killing McGrath?' Randall asked.

For the time it took for Tahoka to walk from his horse until he reached the body, Zococa was silent. He watched the huge Apache scooping the limp body up off the ground in his strong arms. He walked up to the two lawmen.

'He was my friend, *amigo*. He was our friend.'

'I figure Big John Denison and his men did this awful thing to old Giles,' Sheriff Randall heard himself say. 'I ain't figured out why yet, but I still think it was the Double X.'

Zococa watched the huge Indian taking the body out into the shadows.

'I know exactly why Big John

Denison killed Señor Giles.'

'You do?'

'*Sí, amigo.*' Zococa pulled a golden eagle coin from his vest pocket and showed it to both Randall and the shaking Wally Beer.

'I don't understand,' Beer admitted.

'I think maybe I have an inkling of what Zococa means,' Randall said watching the bandit placing the coin between his white teeth and then biting down on it.

Zococa tossed the bent coin into the hands of the sheriff.

'Real gold coins do not bend so easily, but lead ones do.'

'But it looks like gold to me,' Wally Beer said, staring at the coin in the sheriff's hands.

'It's lead, OK. Dipped in gold,' Tobius Randall informed his less bright colleague.

'Exactly, *señor*. This would explain how Denison is so rich he can afford to let his cattle die of old age rather than sell them like other ranchers.'

Zococa noticed flames coming from out in the darkness.

'Big John is making fake coins?' Beer gasped.

'*Sí*. He has been taking real golden eagles and melting them down on the Double X ranch. Then minting lead blanks and dipping them into the gold. For every one real coin I think Denison has managed to make at least five or six counterfeit ones.' Zococa sighed.

'No wonder he didn't want anyone visiting the Double X,' Sheriff Randall snapped.

'What's that big Injun doing to old Giles's body?' Wally Beer nervously asked.

'He is sending Señor Giles to the arms of his God, my short one.' Zococa sighed.

Sheriff Randall edged closer to the bandit. 'I understand McGrath hired you, Zococa.'

'*Sí, amigo.*'

'How much did he pay for your services?'

'He cooked breakfast for my always hungry friend.'

'No money changed hands?' Randall returned the coin back to the thoughtful bandit.

'Señor Giles did not have enough money to hire the great Zococa. So I give him the credit.' Zococa smiled when he saw the figure of Tahoka emerging.

'Why would a wanted outlaw stick his neck out to help a man like McGrath? A man who was almost broke?' Wally Beer asked loudly.

Randall watched as both bandits gathered up their reins and mounted their horses.

'Because he was their friend, Wally.'

Zococa swung his pinto around. It reared up and kicked out at the light of the large moon before its young master looked down at the two lawmen.

'Now it is time for the notorious Zococa to pay Big John Denison a visit,' he said.

'You want company?' the sheriff asked.

'Why would you wish to help a wanted bandit, *señor*?'

'Old Giles happened to be my friend too, son.'

21

The streets of Broken Arrow resounded once more to the crowds of rowdy drinkers and gamblers. For hours they had been unusually quiet as the score of gunfighters who accompanied Big John Denison made their ominous presence felt. Men from both sides of the border tried to keep well clear of the belligerent gang who now sported deputy's stars.

It was only when Denison and his liquored-up men had left the bustling town and headed back to the Double X ranch that the townspeople actually came to life.

A noisy Horseshoe Saloon welcomed the four dusty riders who galloped up to its large front doors. Singing and tinny piano-playing resounded in the night air as they dismounted and stepped up on to the crowded boardwalk.

'I sure hope you're as good with that gun as they say you are, Zococa,' Randall said, looking over the swing doors at the crowded interior of the saloon.

'I am, *señor*.' Zococa placed a thin cigar between his teeth and struck a match along the grip of his pistol.

'You better be, coz I don't relish the idea of taking on Denison or his men with my limited gun-skills.' The sheriff felt a cold shiver enveloping him.

'We gotta get all the rest of the deputies together, Toby. All of them and more,' Wally Beer gushed nervously.

'Hush up. I know that,' Randall said, running the palm of his hand over his face.

Zococa handed his reins to Tahoka as smoke filtered through his teeth.

'Keep our horses in readiness, my little one. We might still need use of them this night.'

Tahoka nodded and watched his

friend lead the sheriff and deputy inside the crowded building. Like a statue the huge warrior stared over the swinging doors watching his friend move through the crowd.

Zococa's keen eyes darted around the room with every step he took towards the long bar. He rested a boot on the brass footrail and then waited for the two lawmen to join him.

'It is a very busy saloon, *señor*,' the bandit remarked.

'Yeah. Too busy for my liking.' Sheriff Randall was ill at ease this night, in a place which was almost his second home.

Zococa raised an eyebrow.

'I think our prey has flown, *amigo*.'

Randall rested a hand on Wally Beer's shoulder and instructed him to gather up as many of their usual posse as he could still find sober enough to ride. The superstitious man rushed into the crowd and disappeared quickly from view.

'Wally's gone looking for my usual

deputies, Zococa.'

'The ones you chased me with?' Zococa grinned at the long mirror as he spoke.

'They ain't that bad.'

'Of course not. Even the greatest posse cannot find Zococa when he does not wish to be found.' Zococa flicked the ash off the end of his cigar and studied the reflected faces of men who were moving around the saloon.

'What'll it be, Sheriff?' one of the bartenders asked.

Randall fought his natural urge to have at least one stiff drink. 'Information. Have you seen Big John Denison around here tonight?'

'Yep. He and that crew of his were here for hours. I'm sure glad they lit out for the Double X though. They were making the rest of my customers nervous,' the barkeep replied.

'When did they leave, *señor*?' Zococa asked through the smoke of his cigar.

The man glanced up at the wall-clock.

'I reckon it must have been about an hour ago that them bastards left town.'

'That means Big John and his cronies should be back at the Double X by now,' Randall said thoughtfully.

'*Sí, amigo.*' The bandit grinned. 'And I do not think he will like what they find.'

'What ya mean?'

'Well, Tahoka and I were a little careless with matches when we discovered the counterfeit golden eagles.' Zococa inhaled deeply on his cigar.

'I don't think I wanna know anything else.' The Sheriff frowned.

Zococa dropped his cigar into a spittoon.

'I think it is time for us to ride for the Double X. But first I think Tahoka and I shall pay a visit to the little round banker who sweats a lot.'

Sheriff Randall gazed across at Wally Beer, who seemed to be having trouble gathering up enough sober men for their posse as the words sank into his tired brain.

'What you want with Chill Weaver, Zococa?'

Zococa's grin widened.

'That, my friend, you would have to be a notorious bandit to understand.'

22

The Texas Mutual Bank was locked up tight. Its bolted doors and barred windows had never been breached in all the days it had stood on the main street of the prosperous Broken Arrow. Not until this night. Until now its defences had always been far superior to any robber's ability to circumvent them.

Chill Weaver had found it impossible to close his eyes to sleep for several days. It had become a total waste of time even bothering to return to his home after he locked the doors of his bank at the end of the working day. Fear was now Weaver's constant companion. Yet it was not the fear of Zococa that twisted like a knife into his guts. It was Big John Denison who filled him with terror.

This terrifying man who had somehow taken control of not only the Texas

Mutual and the fortune held in its vaults, but his own life as well.

Even the bottles of fine whiskey he had consumed seemed incapable of easing his nerves as he finished off yet another bottle and dropped in into the waste bin next to his desk. There was no escape from the shadows of his own imagination.

With bloodshot eyes, the banker reached down into the huge drawer next to his leg and withdrew yet another bottle. Unscrewing the top, Weaver proceeded to pour yet another three fingers of the amber liquid into his glass when a noise from inside the bank itself echoed around his office.

Chill Weaver swallowed the hard liquor and rose swiftly to his feet. For a few seconds the shaking banker did not know what to do next. He had been drinking heavily since the bank closed four hours earlier and suddenly felt the effects reaching his head.

Steadying himself, Weaver slowly pulled the top right-hand drawer of his desk open. The pistol lay where it always lay, on top of a pile of papers. Six spare bullets were next to it. It was a shaking hand that withdrew the gun from its hiding-place and clutched it to his breast.

He could feel his heart pounding against the gun barrel, through his heavily tailored suit. Staggering across his office, Weaver rested his head against the door and listened.

Only silence met his terrified ear.

Weaver gripped the door-handle with his left hand and tried to turn it as quietly as he could. Somehow he managed to enter the huge room silently.

The street lights filtered into the bank through the narrow gaps around the window blinds and traced across the black-and-white chequered flooring up to the wooden tellers'-booths. There was an eerie silence within the building as Weaver followed the gun in his outstretched hand.

Faster than the blink of an eye, the

drunken banker felt something brush before him and realized his gun was no longer in his hand. Weaver stopped in his tracks and turned around to see the perfect white teeth of Zococa flashing at him.

'Zococa!' Weaver exclaimed.

'*Sí*, Señor Weaver. It is I.' Zococa stepped forward and spun the gun on his index finger expertly. 'It is most gratifying to know that you remember me after only one meeting.'

Weaver gulped as he saw the huge Tahoka stepping out of the shadows behind the bandit.

'How did you get in here?' Chill Weaver asked.

'There is no lock which can stop Zococa, *señor*.' Zococa opened the chamber of the pistol and allowed the bullets to fall to the floor at his feet before returning the weapon to the banker.

'What do you want?' Weaver asked, accepting the unloaded gun.

'To do a little business with you,

amigo. Just a little business.'

'What sort of business?'

Zococa produced a golden eagle coin from his jacket pocket and showed it to the sweating man.

'Do you recognize this, *señor*?'

Chill Weaver went silent.

★ ★ ★

Big John Denison had realized that something was dreadfully wrong when he and his score of henchmen had been a mile or more away from the heart of his ranch.

The night sky was as red as blood.

The massive chimney that dominated the Double X courtyard was ablaze with a satanic wrath he had never seen before. Even the stars and moon had been obliterated from view as flames leapt heavenward in an uncontrolled fury.

Something was wrong, Denison thought, as he drove his spurs into the flesh of his exhausted mount and forced it to gallop on towards the inferno. With his highly paid henchmen close at hand, the tall grim-faced rancher rode straight into the courtyard and dragged his lathered-up mount to an abrupt halt.

He could hardly believe his eyes.

There was little left of the building which had sown the seeds of his vast fortune. Most of the massive wooden structure had burned away. Only the brickwork remained as Denison dismounted next to the ranch house.

'Come on men. Help me,' Denison screamed next to the water-trough, searching for a bucket to vainly use on the fire.

His hired gunfighters got off their horses and gathered around the tall raging man.

'It's too late, Big John,' Brad Cutter yelled back through the choking smoke. 'There ain't nothing left to save.'

'Come on, boys. Get some buckets. We can put out this fire if we all work together,' Denison shouted.

His words fell on deaf ears. None of

the gunfighters he had recruited from every cesspit in Texas seemed willing to help now that they could see that the source of his wealth had been razed to the ground.

'What's eating you bastards?' Denison growled angrily.

Brad Cutter walked slowly forward.

'It won't matter how much water we throws on that, Big John. It ain't never gonna be saved. We're just too late.'

Denison clenched both fists and smashed them into the face and body of the smaller man. Cutter hit the ground hard and stayed there as the big man moved towards the others.

'Well?' Denison yelled. 'Anyone else wanna argue?'

Suddenly a voice called from beside the blackened brick wall.

'Big John!'

The tall rancher turned and looked at the kneeling man.

'What you found?'

'A body. It's one of our boys and he's got a bullet hole in him.'

John Denison straightened up and walked towards the man. The others followed. He stared down at the charred corpse and nodded as the kneeling gunman pointed to the bullet hole.

'That's a bullet hole, OK. Who could have done this?'

Brad Cutter staggered to his feet and joined the others.

'I reckon this wasn't no accident, Big John.'

'Zococa!' Denison snorted.

23

Zococa rode at the head of the thirty or more horsemen as they thundered across the Double X grazing land filled with white-faced and longhorn cattle. The ageing beasts scattered in all directions. With the brilliant moon directly overhead and the still-glowing red sky straight in front of the posse, Zococa spurred his magnificent pinto stallion with a fury even he did not fully understand.

Seldom had the Mexican bandit felt the need to seek revenge burning like a fire inside him until now. Yet with every stride his horse took, he recalled the friendly old rancher, Giles McGrath, who had been so brutally cut down on the porch of his own ranch house.

A man who had trusted Zococa to be able to protect him and what was left of his once prosperous cattle ranch.

Perhaps it was guilt that he had failed to do so which drove the young bandit to urge his mount on and on. Whatever the reason, Zococa continued to drive his pinto further and further ahead of the main body of the posse.

Tahoka urged his black gelding on into the centre of the mass of riders but knew his young friend would reach their destination long before his own mount. The massive Apache had never known Zococa so hellbent on vengeance as he was this night.

Sheriff Tobius Randall vainly attempted to keep up with the pinto but knew he too would not be able to match the pace of such a fine stallion.

Zococa allowed his powerful mount to find its own pace and forgot about the other men behind him. He had already drawn and cocked his silver Colt in readiness for what he knew lay over the crest of the hill before him.

He was ready for action.

The bandit drove his mount to the top of the hill and reined in. Zococa screwed up his eyes and stared down into the heart of the Double X compound and the still-burning building. He could see the silhouettes of gunfighters frantically milling about.

As the rest of the posse caught up and drew level with Zococa, it became instantly obvious that Denison and his hired guns had also spotted him.

With all the ferocity of a thunderstorm bullets began to fly up from the Double X compound at the pinto rider and the posse which had gathered around him. White-hot tapers of lethal lead flashed through the riders with deadly accuracy.

At least four of Randall's deputies were plucked from their saddles before the Mexican had time to spur his mount into action and lead the remaining deputies down the hill towards the courtyard of the mysterious Double X.

Faster than any of them had ever ridden before, the riders headed straight into the choking smoke and the cover they knew it would provide.

Rifles and handguns fired from the hired gunfighters all around the towering John Denison. The riders returned each shot with one of their own. Soon the gunsmoke mixed with the acrid swirling black debris from the burning building.

The sound of wounded men resounded within the confines of the large compound. It had taken only a few seconds for the spectre of death to claim its first victims.

Zococa did not wait for his galloping pinto to even slow down when it rounded the long ranch house. The bandit threw himself from the back of the muscular stallion and rolled under the raised boardwalk of the building.

Even though blinded by the billowing smoke of the fire within the furnace, both sides still fanned the hammers of their weapons, intent on nothing less than the total destruction of the opposing force.

Blood seemed to be everywhere as

men fell in all directions.

Sheriff Randall managed to dismount only seconds before a bullet tore through the flesh of his lower left leg. He heard the bone snapping like a dry twig before he crashed heavily down on to the ground.

Even wounded he still managed to aim his guns at Denison's men as they fled from his own deputized riders. With pain tearing through his body, the sheriff had no idea how accurate his bullets were.

Wally Beer somehow managed to locate his fallen friend. He dropped off the back of his own horse and scooped the wounded sheriff up off the cold ground.

'Come on, Toby. I'll get you to cover,' Beer gasped as he struggled with the weight of the older man.

'Leave me, you damn fool,' Randall protested whilst still firing his guns at the men who tried to get closer to them than either cared for. 'Don't risk your own neck.'

Zococa gritted his teeth and crawled beneath the house towards the light of the flames and the sound of dozens of pistols and Winchester rifles.

Reaching the other side of the ranch house, Zococa waited until he could see the figures above him more clearly. Without a moment's hesitation the young bandit leapt from his hiding-place beneath the house and charged at the half-dozen souls who were firing at his fellow posse-riders.

Fanning the hammer of his silver pistol, Zococa hit every one of his targets. Speedily he emptied the spent shells from his gun and filled the steaming chambers with bullets from his black gunbelt. Zococa never stopped moving as his eyes darted all around him.

This was unlike anything the young bandit had ever experienced before.

This was a blood bath.

A war.

Sheriff Randall called out to Zococa. 'Look out behind you, Zococa!'

The Mexican swung around on his heels and focused on the tall figure of John Denison charging towards him with both his guns blazing. Bullets tore through the smoke and ripped into Zococa's black waist-length jacket. The heat of the deadly lead burned through the bandit's white shirt and his skin.

With a speed unmatched by anyone on either side of the border, Zococa raised his left arm and returned fire twice.

The rancher seemed to topple backwards a few paces before steadying himself and then continuing his attack. Blood poured from the snarling Denison as both barrels of his pistols spewed bullets at the bandit. Zococa dropped on to his knees and then felt his sombrero being torn from his head, breaking its drawstring against his chin.

Zococa quickly fired again and this time watched as Denison twisted on his heels and fell heavily into the churned-up ground before him.

'You got Denison, Zococa!' Randall

shouted. Wally Beer helped him walk towards the bandit as he stood upright once more.

'I ain't ever seen such shooting. Such bravery,' Beer gushed in awe of the bandit who was scooping up his sombrero from the ground and inspecting it.

'He shot two holes in my lovely hat, *amigos*,' Zococa complained. 'And look at my jacket. It is ruined.'

Suddenly the shooting all around them seemed to stop as quickly as it had started. The mounted posse rounded up the few remaining gunfighters and herded them towards the wounded sheriff and Zococa.

Brad Cutter was holding his right arm tightly with the fingers of his left hand as blood poured from a massive wound just above his elbow.

'You ain't gonna hang us, is you, Sheriff?' Cutter gasped in agony. 'We was just Big John's hired help.'

Randall spat at the ground.

'You'll have a trial — '

'Then we'll hang you,' Wally Beer interrupted.

Zococa watched as Tahoka rode up to him holding the reins of the pinto stallion.

'Now you arrive, my little rhinoceros? Now all the shooting is ended?'

Tahoka made a few gestures with his hands whilst the bandit stepped into his stirrup and mounted his horse.

'What did he say, son?' Tobius Randall asked.

'He says that he shot at least six of these criminals dead himself, *señor*,' Zococa replied, smiling.

'Six of them, huh?' Beer repeated.

'I think my little *amigo* has been riding with me for far too long. He has started to exaggerate almost as badly as the great Zococa.' The bandit turned his horse around and then pointed at a box near the corner of the ranch house. 'Tahoka and I put that box there earlier, Sheriff. It is full of the counterfeit golden eagles Denison was minting.'

'That's all the proof we need, Zococa. Thanks,' Randall nodded. The two riders spurred their mounts and rode off towards Broken Arrow again.

'Is that what all this has been about, Sheriff?' Beer asked the lawman.

'Find my horse. I gotta get back to town and get this busted leg fixed, Wally,' Randall sighed.

Finale

It was nearly eleven when Zococa and Tahoka rode back into the still-busy streets of Broken Arrow. The two riders allowed their mounts to move slowly until they reached the small cantina they had visited when they had first arrived in town.

'I think you must be very hungry by now, little one,' Zococa said to the stony-faced Apache. Tahoka nodded.

Zococa dismounted and handed his companion a few gleaming silver dollars. 'You go in and buy as much food and wine as you want.'

Tahoka turned his friend around and used his hands to speak to him.

Zococa patted the face of the huge Apache. 'Do not fret. I have a little business to finish; that is all. I shall join you in ten minutes or so.'

Tahoka inhaled the aromatic delights

of the food which came through the swaying beaded curtain of the cantina and reluctantly nodded before entering the open doorway.

Zococa bit his lower lip and moved quickly along the narrow lanes until he reached the back of the Texas Mutual Bank. With the agility of a puma, he climbed up the rear wall and soon located the skylight on the sloping roof. Within seconds he had opened it and silently entered the building.

True to his word, Zococa's business had only taken five minutes when he left the bank by a side doorway. The dark lane was quiet and yet a mere hundred feet further down the narrow thoroughfare was the boisterous Horseshoe Saloon. Zococa began to retrace his steps along the dark lane when for some reason he paused to look over his shoulder. The sight that met his eyes stopped him in his tracks.

They say that curiosity killed the cat. It was a curious sight that drew

Zococa along the lane and out into the main street.

Tied up next to a dozen or more other horses next to the Horsehoe Saloon, Zococa had spotted a fine pinto stallion in full livery. For a brief moment he had thought it was his own mount but knew that was unlikely as he had left it tied up outside the cantina.

Walking closer to the fine animal, Zococa realized that this stallion was marked slightly differently from his own fine pinto. He recalled the people of San Pueblo telling him of another man who visited their remote village. He too rode a pinto stallion.

Curiosity had hooked Zococa like a fish.

The bandit stood next to the horse and ran a knowledgeable hand along its neck.

'You are a handsome devil but not as handsome as my own horse I think,' Zococa said to the nervous horse.

Suddenly Zococa felt a cold shiver tracing his spine. He became aware of the three armed men who were standing in the shadows around him.

Slowly, the bandit turned and caught sight of the faces above the glowing cigars. Haunting faces. These men were not simple visitors to Broken Arrow. They had a reason to be in town.

He was that reason.

'You are bounty hunters, *amigos*?' Zococa asked as he moved cautiously away from the string of horses until he was standing in the centre of the street.

'We are not bounty hunters, Zococa,' an elegant voice announced as the tallest of the three men edged out of the blackness and stepped down into the street to face the bandit.

'Then what?' Zococa was still curious.

'We are agents from the Emperor, Zococa,' Orlando Fernandez said. He drained the last inch of smoke from his cigar and dropped it on to the sand. 'I am Colonel Fernandez and these are two of my best men.'

'The Emperor?' Zococa grinned.

'What does his Excellency want of Zococa, *señor?*'

'He wants you dead,' Fernandez replied coldly.

From the corners of his eyes, Zococa could see the other two men emerging from the shadows to either side of him.

'I take it the fine pinto stallion belonged to someone that you mistook for myself?' Zococa flexed his fingers, never taking his eyes off the man directly in front of him.

'A slight error,' Fernandez shrugged. 'One which we will not repeat now that we have found you.'

'You wish to kill Zococa? But why?'

'Your head will bring us a fortune.'

Zococa raised his eyebrows.

'I do not like the idea of being separated from my head, *señor*. I have grown so used to it.' Zococa could see his humour was falling on deaf ears. These men were serious. Deadly serious.

'You may attempt to draw your

weapon,' Fernandez nodded. 'Then we will kill you.'

Zococa swallowed hard. 'You are most kind.'

Suddenly to Zococa's right, Jose Remo gave a huge gasp and staggered from the shadows in front of a hardware store. He fell headlong off the boardwalk into the street.

Orlando Fernandez's eyes flashed at his dead cohort and then spotted the gleaming knife in the hand of the huge figure of Tahoka who had just emerged from the dark lane.

'The heathen!' Fernandez screamed across to Carlos Concisco. 'Kill the heathen!'

Before Concisco could obey his orders, Tahoka threw the heavy knife across the width of the street. The blade sank to its hilt into the man's chest. Concisco managed to squeeze his trigger once before toppling off the boardwalk and landing in a trough.

Fernandez drew his pistol swiftly. His speed was matched only by that of

Zococa. Both men fanned the hammers of their weapons at exactly the same time and both bullets found their targets within a split second of leaving their barrels.

The colonel was lifted off his feet and thrown backwards as Zococa's deadly aim once more proved true. Yet Tahoka watched in horror as his young friend was also hit and knocked off his own feet by an equally accurate shot.

Before the giant Apache had even started to rush to the assistance of Zococa, the bandit had landed on his back heavily in the sandy street.

Tahoka knelt down over his fallen friend and stared in total disbelief at the sight. For a few seconds there was silence.

Then Zococa coughed and looked up at the startled warrior who bore down on him. Zococa blinked and then patted his chest. The sound of coins could be heard.

Tahoka pulled back the black lapel of Zococa's jacket to reveal a bag hanging over his heart on a string which went around the back of the bandit's neck and was joined to another bag full of golden coins on his right side.

The hands of Tahoka asked for an explanation.

'Do not worry, little one. I think the golden eagles our friend the banker gave me to be silent about his dealings with Denison have saved my life.'

Tahoka pulled the bandit back on to his feet. Zococa stared at the hole in his jacket.

'I must buy some new clothes. I have bullet holes in practically everything I'm wearing.'

The huge Indian shook his head as the pair walked back into the lane and headed for the cantina and their horses. Zococa patted the wide back of his friend.

'Gracious, *amigo*.'

It was a mere twenty minutes later when Zococa and Tahoka rode their mounts through the twisting back-streets of Broken Arrow on their way to the nearby border. Zococa gripped a long thin cigar between his teeth and puffed thoughtfully as they rode beneath the balcony he recognized as belonging to the very beautiful female named Rita.

Zococa stopped his pinto and stared up at the open doorway high above them. Tahoka touched the sleeve of the young bandit and shook his head.

'Be silent, my little one. Can you not hear the soft bosom of the lovely Rita heaving as she dreams of making love to the great Zococa?'

Tahoka made urgent signals with his hands.

'What is wrong? This young female desires only to have me make love to her. Am I so heartless that I would ignore her desperate pleas?'

The Apache pointed up at the window again. This time the expression on his face spoke far more loudly than his sign language ever could.

Zococa stood in his stirrups and stared up at the balcony.

'Rita, my darling little one. Are you there?'

Suddenly Zococa's eyes widened as he saw the double-barrel scattergun being poked over the balcony and aimed down at him. The face of a middle-aged man with gritted teeth was staring angrily down its sights.

'So you're Zococa, are ya? The swine who ravished my little daughter? I've been waiting for you to come back.'

'It was only a little ravishing, *señor*.'

'I'll kill ya!'

'Ride, Tahoka!' Zococa shouted to his friend. Without a second's hesitation they both spurred their mounts and headed down the street at full gallop. Both riders heard the blast of the scattergun behind them but did not slow their pace until they had reached the river.

'Is it not strange how some men simply do not like having their daughters make love to Zococa, little one?' Zococa asked as a smile crossed his handsome features once more. 'I would think they would be honoured.'

Tahoka followed the laughing rider across the shallow river back into Mexico.

'Still, we have much money now, Tahoka.' Zococa patted the bags of coins hanging around his neck. 'That means much food for you and many more pretty girls for me.'

Zococa's roaring laughter drifted over the crystal-clear water as the pair disappeared into the moonlit woods.

We do hope that you have enjoyed reading this large print book.

Did you know that all of our titles are available for purchase?

We publish a wide range of high quality large print books including:
Romances, Mysteries, Classics
General Fiction
Non Fiction and Westerns

Special interest titles available in large print are:
The Little Oxford Dictionary
Music Book, Song Book
Hymn Book, Service Book

Also available from us courtesy of Oxford University Press:
Young Readers' Dictionary
(large print edition)
Young Readers' Thesaurus
(large print edition)

For further information or a free brochure, please contact us at:
Ulverscroft Large Print Books Ltd.,
The Green, Bradgate Road, Anstey,
Leicester, LE7 7FU, England.
Tel: (00 44) 0116 236 4325
Fax: (00 44) 0116 234 0205

THE CHISELLER

Tex Larrigan

Soon the paddle steamer would be on its long journey down the Missouri River to St Louis. Now, all Saul Rhymer had to do was to play the last master stroke of the evening. He looked at the mounting pile of gold and dollar bills and again at the cards in his hand. Then, looking around the table, he produced the deed to the goldmine in Montana. 'Let's play poker!' But little did he know how that journey back to St Louis would change his life so drastically.

THE ARIZONA KID

Andrew McBride

When former hired gun Calvin Taylor took the job of sheriff of Oxford County, New Mexico, it was for one reason only — to catch, or kill, the notorious Arizona Kid, and pick up the fifteen hundred dollars reward the governor had secretly offered. Taylor found himself on the trail of the infamous gang known as the Regulators, hunting down a man who'd once been his friend. The pursuit became, in every sense, a journey of death.

BULLETS IN BUZZARDS CREEK

Bret Rey

The discovery of a dead saloon girl is only the beginning of Sheriff Jeff Gilpin's problems. Fortunately, his old friend 'Doc' Holliday arrives in Buzzards Creek just as Gilpin is faced by an outlaw gang. In a dramatic shoot-out the sheriff kills their leader and Holliday's reputation scares the hell out of the others. But it isn't long before the outlaws return, when they know Holliday is not around, and Gilpin is alone against six men . . .

THE YANKEE HANGMAN

Cole Rickard

Dan Tate was given a virtually impossible task: to save the murderer Jack Williams from the condemned cell. Williams, scum that he was, held a secret that was dear to the Confederate cause. But if saving Williams would test all Dan's ingenuity, then his further mission called for immense courage and daring. His life was truly on the line and if he didn't succeed, Horace Honeywell, the Yankee Hangman would have the last word!